A SPRING KILL

THE KILLING SEASONS
BOOK 2

JK ELLEM

"The best revenge is not to be like your enemy."
—Marcus Aurelius Antoninus, 121AD - 180AD.

"Bullshit."
—Carolyn Ryder, now.

A SPRING KILL

1

MY DEATH "TO-DO" LIST

I turn my head sideways and look at the image on the screen, to the blemish, no bigger than a dime, that's going to kill me.

We are all going to die—eventually. I almost did, recently, in some dark, snowbound plain in Iowa. But I cheated death that frozen winter night at the hands of a very determined, ruthless killer. I kept fighting back until his murderous grip released me, and he receded into his own deathly darkness at the hands of my new lifelong friend while I lost two pints of blood before slipping into a two-week coma.

But I survived, and so had Beau Hodges.

And now? It is an entirely different matter. This...thing that's growing inside my head, too close to my brain, I cannot cheat.

So I've been told.

I can't even run from it because, wherever I go, it comes along for the ride, a cancerous remora clinging to me, feeding on what precious life I have left, growing and getting stronger while I'm surely going to get weaker in the coming months.

So I've been told.

"How many months?" I hear myself ask as I lie on the examination table, with the oncologist, dressed in a white coat, hovering over me.

She tells me nine months, maybe twelve at the most, if I start treatment immediately.

Twelve months at the most.

I've never been an optimist, always the pessimist. That's why I'm good at my job. Let's stick with nine months, not twelve, shall we? Let's add some urgency to an already urgent situation.

It's March, the start of spring, and from what I've been told, I have three seasons left on this earth to enjoy. And yet so much to do, but only one thing that truly needs to be done. I'm determined to get to the fall—before I eventually fall from this earth. Can I stretch it to twelve months?

It's a very big "maybe."

I could pause, I guess, take stock, reflect on what could've been. Get my minimal affairs in order. Do what is expected upon hearing such news. Make amends, perhaps forgive those I haven't forgiven, even if they don't deserve it. Isn't that what you do in moments like this? Isn't that what should be going through your head? Compile a Before I Die to-do list?

I think about those words again as I stand outside the clinic, on the sidewalk, people swirling around me like fish in a stream, and traffic slipping left and right, up and down the street.

Life goes on, but apparently mine isn't going to.

Nine months.

I tilt my face and enjoy the warm, sweet morning sunshine, and yet cold black thoughts leave a bitterness in my mind. I've defied the odds all my life, all thirty years of it. I was born eight weeks premature and given only a forty percent chance of surviving; was hit by a drunk driver when I was eight years old while riding my bike on the sidewalk; been shot twice; hit with a crossbow bolt, nearly bled to death, and technically died on the operating table. And I've had my heart broken. And now I have just three more seasons, so I've been told, maybe four, to live.

Stop right there, Carolyn! You said, let's not be too optimistic;

let's add some urgency to the ticking clock. Okay. My mistake. Nine months, not twelve.

Anyway, as I was saying to myself, in all my thirty years, I've never done what was expected of me. And I'm certainly not going to start now.

I take the radiation therapy referral that's in my hand, scrunch it up into a tight ball with my clenched fist, then toss it into the nearest trash can.

And as I'm walking away, I think about fall and all the colors of the leaves and how beautiful it's going to be.

It's all going to end one way or another.

And as far as my Before I Die to-do list is concerned? Fuck that!

There's only one thing on my to-do list, and it has been there for the past six months. There is true evil out there in the world, the devil incarnate. I've crossed paths with him a few times, and each time, the slippery bastard has managed to escape and gone on—with this particular killing spree—to leave a trail of dead women in his heinous, depraved wake. And if I don't stop him, no one else will.

No, God can wait. She'll understand. I have important work still to do down here on earth before I go to wherever the hell you go when you die. First, I need to walk through the valley of darkness and find him, the Highway Killer.

Samuel-fucking-Pritchard.

2

THE HEALING WOMAN

He came at me with a knife, so I sent him away in the back of an ambulance with a broken wrist, a fractured cheekbone, and a wound requiring several stitches in the ER, I was told.

All this for a few dollars in my purse—hardly worth being mugged for—and all under the pretense that I would be easy prey for him. Maybe it was how I looked after leaving the clinic, walking listlessly to my car. Vulnerable. Distracted. Admittedly, I was lost in my own thoughts, hadn't seen the mugger step out of the alleyway, knife in hand, a rabid snarl across his face.

Then I just lost it, saw him as the vessel for my sudden outpouring of anger and resentment at the news I had just been given. Up until then I'd been fine, in control, my mind absent of questions of self-pity like, Why me? Or, I don't deserve this.

Thankfully, the local police agreed that my response had been proportionate, measured, not excessive, although they were a little surprised by my ability to inflict such damage on a much larger male attacker.

After a statement was given, and forms were ticked, I was free to go. I then retreated to the beach house I'm renting, high up on the bluff, overlooking the bay. I had sold my apartment in Salt Lake City, adding the money to my share of my mother's estate from selling the family home in Willow Falls, Iowa. Combined with my own savings, I have more than enough to do what needs to be done, to follow it through to the very end—no matter what. A steroid-jacked street thug is not going to derail my plans. I've dealt with worse, much worse, including having been hunted by one of the most ruthless predators known, Robin Hood, the infamous winter serial killer—and had survived. But I didn't tell the local police that.

My sister Jodie, who still lives in Willow Falls, I don't want to burden with my bad news. She'll only try to convince me to return to Iowa. It's not my home, just a town filled with unpleasant memories. She wouldn't understand this path I've embarked on either. I will tell her, eventually.

On most days I'm up early. Following the winding, sun-bleached wooden stairs at the rear of the property, I descend the bluff, passing over the treacherous black rocks below, before setting foot on the small deserted beach.

Wrapped in a shawl but barefoot—I love the feeling of the cold, wet sand between my toes—I imagine I cut a lonely figure as I walk along the glistening water's edge, staying the course, sloshing ankle-deep through the cold foam of the waves. And as the water recedes with a rasping hiss, my footsteps vanish behind me.

The days are growing longer now. The sun rising a little earlier, the smoldering orange coals of dusk appearing a little later in the western sky, the gentle ocean breeze a little warmer, chasing away the last of the winter chills that I felt during the past months. The salt air, clear skies, and the warmth of the sun is the best medicine for me to recuperate, to heal as best I can. My right shoulder has fully mended, leaving only a nickel-sized purple blemish in my skin where the crossbow bolt had entered.

I can now do twenty chin-ups on the galvanized pipe I rigged up between the hardwood posts on the back porch and feel no ill-effects from the two broken ribs I had suffered. Eighty crunches—ten more than my previous best—is the next goal I've set for myself.

The right wrist is another matter entirely. It is fine, if "fine" is good enough—but it's not. Not for me and what I need to finish.

The bones of the wrist still make an incessant clicking sound whenever I tilt my hand vertically up or down. As annoying as it is, it doesn't stop me from drawing my handgun from its holster in under one second and squeezing the trigger during my daily dry-firing sessions that I do in the garage, hidden from view. Privacy is what I crave during this time. Mind you, the closest neighbor is at least a mile away along the bluff.

At night, after a simple dinner, taken on the back porch, I venture down into the basement, pausing at the foot of the stairs to briefly enjoy the trapped warmth of the day that still lingers there. Then, stepping across the threshold and into the small storage room that I have converted into an office, the atmosphere changes in a heartbeat, and I'm transported into another world, far from the daytime world I restlessly roam. This other world is full of pain, suffering, unimaginable evil, and where a distinct coldness lays its heavy hands on my shoulders whenever I visit. It is my burden, my choice to be there, in that room each night, for no one else is going to help these lost souls.

During this nightly vigil, I always carry my handgun in the waistband of my sweatpants, a round in the chamber. I can't explain why, except that on more than one occasion, while hunched in front of my computer at night, with the house locked securely above, I would turn and glance back over my shoulder to the foot of the basement stairs, expecting to see him standing there.

During these dark, quiet hours spent in this room, I reacquaint myself with the dead, all those women who, over the months, I have grown to know intimately. I religiously study my "murder map," a murderous trail of small towns and communities, of bodies and body parts as I closely follow in the footsteps of those who have gone before.

Brenda O'Donnell, single mother and waitress, from Springfield, Illinois, found dismembered in a culvert under the railroad tracks, not two hundred yards from the diner where she worked sixty hours a week to put food on the table and her only son through college.

Mary Bickford, mother of three, found in a shallow grave beside a roadside picnic spot.

Lottie Carlson, the high school tenth grader whose body has yet to be found. She had gone missing on the short walk home from class. Her backpack was found discarded fifty miles upstate on the side of the highway.

Then there is Bobby Lee Granger, the odd one out. The thirty-three-year-old highway patrol officer whom I believe followed a little too closely in the wake of evil before she knew what she was truly dealing with.

I hypothesize that she had gotten close, had touched it, unintentionally disturbing it. And for her sins, she ended up in the trunk of her police cruiser, her throat cut so deep the medical examiner commented in his autopsy report that her head and neck resembled a Pez candy dispenser.

And when I look east, toward where the Potomac River gently laps the banks of Virginia, I know there is another, a man who is on this same hunt as me, following in the same murderous footsteps of evil. This man also has a map on his wall, dotted with small red pins, moving west to east, marking shallow roadside graves, a cave, desolate parking lots in national state forests and other dumping grounds along lonely back roads.

I've found no solace in this place where I work until the small hours of the morning. Just a limitless supply of anguish to feed my determination to catch him, my nemesis: the man who haunts me endlessly. The man who has evaded me once before. The man who tried to kill me.

So, I made a vow, that I am going to find him first, before the fall, before my heart stops beating, before God gives up on me.

And he will surely die before I do.

That is my vow, not to myself, but to all those he has already taken from this earth.

3

PRITCHARD

He was three miles to the west of her, and she had no clue the devil was that close, just over the flat horizon, pulled up on the side of a desolate stretch of highway.

It was almost as if he could smell her: young, blonde, and ripe for the killing. Looking east, his wizened eyes squinted off into the distance and he licked his lips. She was there, beyond the watery shimmer of the spring morning. Not a mirage, but warm, vibrant flesh, pulsing blood, and growing bone, for him to take, to taste, then to break into a million sorrowful pieces.

He leaned against the hood of the pickup truck and contemplated his next move. It had been a while, almost six months now since his last, a spritely young server at a truck stop diner. He had watched her finish her shift that clear, cool night as she walked across the parking lot behind the diner, sashaying her hips, her blonde ponytail swaying side to side behind the beautiful curve of her skull.

As he watched, he imagined taking a pry bar to her head, cracking open the cranium like an ostrich egg, seeing the spongy gray yolk ooze out across her smooth forehead, then down her pretty little face. He could smell her too that night, as he stood in the shadows between the two big rigs. That sweet, musty smell of womanly spice and all things nice wafted in the cool breeze from her tight, young beaver. It fascinated him how they all smelled slightly different, yet they all had the same effect on the men around them, like a bitch in heat, oozing pheromones to attract all the neighborhood strays.

No security cameras, pitiful lighting, plenty of shadows, and a twenty-year-old hatchback with a good old-fashioned metal key, not a fob, that required a few precious extra seconds for her to stop, insert, then twist before unlocking her car door.

It was all too easy.

He had already picked out the spot to take her where privacy was assured. It was an old, abandoned gas station just off the highway a few miles from the diner where she worked. Secluded, desolate, unnoticed by uncaring eyes. A quiet place where he could enjoy her slow, brutal destruction. He had noticed the place when he had driven past it before happening on the truck stop, farther along the highway from where he had pulled in.

Boarded up with ply, sagging and sorrowful, it was a perfect den of debauchery for him to do as he wished with her. It was always the same for him. He would always stumble upon a place first, then find a woman to occupy it. And careless women were easy to find. He wasn't open to quick kills in darkened alleys, or back seats, or derelict yards. The threat of discovery was always too great.

No. He wanted to linger over them. Wanted to savor their fear, their delicious flesh, for hours, even days. The devil wasn't one to be rushed. This was his kingdom, his domain. The wide-open highways. The small, long-forgotten towns. And he had all the time in the world.

However, there was that female police officer. That, unfortunately, was a quick kill and totally out of character for him. She was clever, pulled him over and fixed him with a gaze of suspicion for some lame traffic infringement. Wanting to search the back cab of his pickup was her eventual downfall. So, as he kindly opened the door, and while she had leaned in to look, he hastened her journey to the afterlife with six inches of steel that he slipped into the base of her skull. Slitting her throat after piling her into the trunk of her own police cruiser was just a theatrical afterthought. He could have easily left her on the side of the road to rot in the blazing sun.

Blinking hard, he shook off his trip down memory lane and came back to the present, his eyes focusing on a spot in the distance.

Yes. She was there.

Pushing himself off the pickup's hood, he climbed in and started the engine, and with a throaty roar from the V8 and churn of grit and stone under the meaty tires, he pulled off the dirt shoulder and back onto the blacktop and accelerated...toward her.

4

EMMA

It wasn't as though she'd done anything wrong by taking her mom's car and wanting to see her father after he had walked out on them eighteen years ago.

Her mother, Karen, had said her father was a no-good bum, had walked out just six months after Emma had been born. Unable to cope with the pressure of unexpected fatherhood, Billy Block had fled the family trailer-park home, made off with a local woman who was a cleaner, and was never seen or heard of again.

For most of Emma's eighteen years of life, her mother had told her very little about her father except that he was a good-for-nothing diesel mechanic she'd met in a bar in Reno, who promptly bedded her that same night. And the result? Emma Block, weighing in at a premature four pounds three ounces after an emergency cesarean.

For almost three months, Emma Karen Block knew nothing of the real world outside the soundless plastic shell of her incubator chamber. But Emma was a fighter, the doctors and nurses had told Karen during the daily vigil she spent by her daughter's side. Defying the odds, and with tubes thrust down her nose and throat, baby Emma clung to life with both of her tiny hands. Soon she began to grow, a little at first, almost unnoticeably by her mother who watched on, day after day, never leaving Emma's side, hoping and praying that her little Emma would survive. And God answered her prayers in the form of a few additional ounces of added weight to Emma's fragile body after the second week. Emma grew stronger, more determined, until finally the tubes were removed, and Karen was able to truly hold her daughter in her arms for the first time.

Billy only visited Emma once in the hospital before she was discharged, said something uncomplimentary to Karen about poor maternal genetics and then stayed away.

The first few months at home with Emma were tough for Karen, and Billy offered no help whatsoever. He had a job at a local garage, working on big haulers, and seemed to return home later and later each night, his breath reeking of alcohol and other women. But Karen relished the time spent alone with her daughter, just the two of them. It also allowed her to contemplate the broader picture that precluded a loving, attentive, committed husband and father to Emma.

It did worry Karen, however, that with just one income coming in, she would be left to fend for herself, with a newborn, and would need to find a way to put food on the table and diapers in the drawer, should Billy decide to leave. And he did, three months later.

Never one to dwell on life's curveballs, Karen Block saw his leaving as a new beginning, a major reset in her life. Undeterred, she scrimped what little money she had, and, borrowing a neighbor's laptop, did an online bookkeeping course. Then she took a job doing the books for the trailer park's owner, all the while keeping a watchful eye on Emma in a cot by her side in her own trailer. Soon, she had enough money to upgrade to a larger trailer, and then she bought a small sedan because Billy had taken their only ride.

For the next eighteen years, both mother and daughter flourished. They needed no one else in their lives.

That was until a week shy of Emma's eighteenth birthday, when a cheap Hallmark card arrived. Seemed like Karen wasn't the only one keeping track of Emma's birthdays. After all these years, Billy now wanted back into Emma's life. Typical, Karen thought when she secretively peeled open the envelope and read the card. She'd done all the hard work as a single mother, working two jobs while raising Emma. And now, Billy wanted to swan back into their lives and suddenly become a family all over again.

Yeah, right.

On the card was a cell phone number, and mother and daughter had argued. Emma wanted to meet her father, while a distraught Karen strictly forbade it, almost wishing she had torn up the card without Emma knowing. This morning, Emma took her mom's car keys, packed a bag, and left the trailer park before dawn and before Karen woke, and called her father who gave her the details of a motel where he was staying. What she didn't expect was the Honda Civic breaking down in the middle of nowhere on the way to meeting him.

Emma leaned under the hood of the Honda Civic and squinted at the hissing engine, unsure of what she was looking at or why the fifteen-year-old hatchback had developed a sudden coughing, spluttering fit before she coasted it to the dirt shoulder of the road before the car had died completely under her, the dash then exploding with red warning lights.

She checked her cell phone. No credit left. "Damn it!" she cursed. Stepping back, she glanced along both directions of the desolate stretch of highway.

Nothing.

If only her father were here now, he'd know what to do. The address he'd given her was a place perhaps under five miles away. The car had plenty of gas, so it must be something wrong with the engine.

Maybe she could hitchhike, get to a phone booth or perhaps a good Samaritan would stop and let her use their cell phone so she could call him. Her mother would be fretting right now, knowing that Emma had taken the car for one purpose only. And why shouldn't Emma see her father? She knew nothing of him. It wasn't like she was walking out on her mom either. Emma planned to just meet with him, see what he was like, then return home. She had a ton of questions she wanted to ask, especially why he had walked out on both her and her mother when she was just a baby.

Was she angry? A little. More curious about whom he was more than anything.

Emma gave the engine one last glare before stepping back and searching the horizon again. Nothing seemed to be moving out there amid the flat, rippling landscape.

She checked her cell again. Nothing. *Christ*! It was no use. She would just have to wait until a car passed by and try her best to hitch a ride.

Twenty minutes later, a dark shimmering speck wobbled in the watery distance along the highway.

Wearing cut-off shorts and a tank top, Emma knew she cast an attractive picture. Shielding her eyes, she watched as the speck grew. It was a vehicle of some sort, and thankfully it was heading straight for her.

She smiled.

It seemed like her luck was changing.

5

TAKEN

A large, dark pickup truck materialized along the highway, then pulled up a short distance behind where the Honda Civic had broken down.

The driver's side window powered down, and a cool slice of air hit Emma's face as she climbed up onto the sidestep next to the door and peered inside the cabin.

A man sat behind the wheel, mid-sixties perhaps, short, bristly gray hair, kind eyes, his frame heavyset, with powerful shoulders and firm hands that gripped the steering wheel.

"Need a hand, little lady?"

Relief washed over her. Finally, someone to help her so she wouldn't be stuck on this damn road. "Thanks." She gestured toward the Civic. "Not sure what happened. It just kinda died. Plenty of gas in it."

The man angled his head to look outside, then nodded before grabbing something off the seat beside him. Probably his cell phone, Emma thought.

"Let me take a look," he said, his gaze dropping back on Emma.

While he had kind eyes, they were a piercing gray that made her feel like they were drilling into Emma's head, probing deep into her soul. He didn't seem harmful, though, but Emma couldn't shake the tinge of trepidation that had suddenly settled on her. She shrugged it off as her just being overly cautious. Ever since she was a child, she had an inherent ability to look past people's initial first impressions and see their true intentions. Maybe it was because of her mother constantly drumming it into her about men and the ulterior motives they all have, just to get into your pants. Emma blamed her mom's deep-seated bitterness toward her father for walking out on them as the reason for her general view on all males.

"Sure," Emma said, climbing down from the sidestep. "That would be great." She glanced back down both sides of the long stretch of desolate highway.

The man unbuckled his seat belt, slid out, and she followed behind him as he made his way toward the front of the Honda, where the hood was still latched up. He placed his large hands on the lip of the engine bay and looked inside before giving a solemn, "Hmmm."

Concern flared in Emma's mind, and her heart sank. "What's wrong with it?"

"Looks like you've got some real engine trouble here," he said over his shoulder while reaching inside the engine bay with one hand.

Great, Emma thought. She had no money to get the car towed, if that's what was needed. "Can you fix it?" she asked, hopefully, knowing with her luck it would be unlikely.

"Maybe." He leaned farther in and gave his chin a rub. "I know a few things about engines. I do much of my own work on my own vehicles. I've got some tools back in my truck."

That sounded promising to Emma. And yet as she watched him hunched over the engine bay, she couldn't shake the unsettling feeling that was growing inside her. His words sounded genuine yet felt laced with something else, seemed too contrived, theatrical, like he was reading words from a script, playing the concerned good Samaritan.

The sun passed behind a bank of clouds, and the daylight dimmed slightly. Emma felt a chill ripple across her bare shoulders, and she rubbed them with both her hands. "Hey, look, maybe if I could just use your cell phone, call someone to come and get me," she said.

"Well, now," the man drawled, ignoring her comment and pulling back slightly from the engine bay. "Would ya look at that?"

Hesitantly, Emma shuffled forward to look to where he was now pointing. "What?"

"Ya see that cable there?" he continued, swiveling his head toward her. "Take a look-see."

A wedge of shadow from the raised hood had fallen across the innards of the engine bay, making it impossible for Emma to see what he was pointing at. "Where?" she asked, moving closer until she was standing next to him, shoulder to shoulder. He was a good foot taller than her.

"Right there," he replied, pointing into the dark interior. "That yellow cable. You see it?"

Holding her hair back with one hand, Emma leaned in some more and squinted at where he was pointing.

"Well, there's your problem right there." He chuckled, shuffling his feet slightly.

Emma leaned farther in. "I can't see anything." And that was the truth, just the engine block, rubber hoses, and a tangle of wires. Certainly not the yellow cable he was referring to.

"Right there," the man insisted. "You can't miss it."

Emma jerked her head up as cold fear, icy as chilled water, dribbled down her spine. His voice had shifted from being next to her, to being...*behind*.

A powerful, tentacle-like arm wrapped around her chest, pinning both her arms to her sides, and a damp piece of gauze was pressed hard over her nose and mouth. A cloying, stringent smell flooded her airways. Horror, sickly warm and foul, filled Emma as he whispered into her ear, "You're mine now. All mine."

Darkness came fast after that, seeping in from the edges of her eyes before cutting off all light a few heartbeats later.

6

DARK WOODS

A thick blanket of mist and fog covers the ocean and shoreline below, and the morning sky is an endless deep blue. I can hear the constant crash, then the rasp of the waves below me, stealing grains of sand little by little. And just like the ebb and flow of the waves, whatever I try to push away from my mind always ends up getting pulled back to the forefront.

The trail rims the cliff tops, drifting too close to the edge in some places and not close enough in others. It feels great to be outside this time of the day, my stomach empty, my mind clear.

Parts of the cliff edge have slid away, fallen to the beach hundreds of feet below, leaving huge clawlike tears in the earth, exposing layers of soil and rock to the sun and wind for the first time.

I check my GPS watch. I'm a mile out from my beach house, running hard, my eyes scanning the ever-changing terrain in front of me, searching out dips and grooves, rocks partially hidden, or old tree roots keen to trip me up. As I crest a small rise, a house comes into view in the distance. My closest neighbor. He's an author, I've been told by some of the townsfolk. Each year, he comes in the spring and stays until the fall to finish his new book. On my daily jogs, I've never seen him, and the house always looks deserted whenever I pass it by, never stopping to take note.

But today I do, pausing at the small path that leads to a low, leaning wood-and-wire fence at the rear of the property. The house is a yellow-painted, gabled, wraparound-porch affair, with white shutters and a solitary chair on the back deck. A car, electric by the looks of it, is parked in the dirt driveway at the side. I mask my observations with some casual stretching, stealing glances at the place every few seconds.

But then my curiosity wanes, and I move off again, increasing my pace, leaving the house on the cliff and its invisible occupant behind me.

Cutting inland, the trail soon dips down, and I plunge into the thicket of trees, a small, wooded area. Shadows spring up around me, and coldness touches my skin. The scent of pine needles fills my senses. Over logs, around hollow stumps and branches, I duck and weave, ferns brushing at my shins, then trudge across a small stream, my Gore-Tex running shoes splashing through the cold water, pebbles crunching underfoot as I run as though being chased by something.

The trail rises, and I burst out into brilliant sunshine on the other side. My heart darkens, as it always does whenever I see what's up ahead, a place of bad memories. I could avoid it, bypass the spot, and run a wider loop. But I don't, and I'm unsure why. Just as you must confront your fears, you also must vanquish your regrets.

The trail curves back toward the cliff edge, to where a gnarly lone cypress stands on a granite outcrop of jagged rock. On good days, I ignore it, continue running past, my vision focused on the path ahead. On bad days, my feet seem to drag themselves to a halt on their own accord, and I can't avoid staring at the piece of rope dangling from a thickly twisted branch that protrudes out over the abyss. The end of the rope is frayed from where it snapped. I weigh more now. Less fat, more muscle. Less doubt, more self-belief.

Today is one of those good days. So, I continue past the lone cypress, accelerating as I do. But it's there, a sinister blemish always looming in the periphery of my mind. A memory that I can never scrub away.

Ten minutes later, I reach the turnaround point, the tip of the headland, where the coastline cuts back inland before curving down and around to where the Township of Erin's Bay hugs a crescent-shaped coastline in the salt-hazed distance.

The last of the mist and fog has gone, burned off by the rising temperature and radiant sunshine. I slow, then stop completely. Turning, I glance behind me from where I've come. I've seen no one else up here, jogging or otherwise. A strong breeze ruffles my hair across my face, and my top, damp and cold with sweat, clings to my skin. The windswept headland is empty. Not a soul in sight.

After a few stretches, I head back, faster this time, going around the woods instead of through them. It takes longer, but I don't care. By the time I arrive back at my place, adrenaline is coursing through me, and my chest and lungs throb.

Inside, I peel off my clothes while glancing at my nightstand to where a well-thumbed copy of the Australian classic, *Picnic at Hanging Rock*, which I found in a thrift store in Erin's Bay, sits open. I've only just recently discovered reading again simply for the joy of it, and for my mind to "shift gears" at the end of the day. Red wine helps, too, paired with dark chocolate.

After a shower, I take a cup of freshly brewed coffee out onto the back porch and sit down in the full sun. My doctor said I have vitamin D deficiency. So, I try to catch at least half an hour of full sunlight each day before it gets too warm. It seems pointless, yet I'm sure I will look much better with a suntan when I'm eventually lying in my casket.

Drinking my coffee, I think about my funeral service, wondering who will attend. My phone dings, and I look at the screen. My heart quickens as I read the brief text.

C, girl gone missing. Could be something. See attached. BV.

7

NIGHTMARE

Emma woke, startled and confused, her memory foggy, like a piece of it was missing, her eyes blurry, crusted over, and a thumping ache behind the bridge of her nose, like her brain was trapped inside a whistling pressure cooker.

She tried to remember. Something about an old man with kind eyes. *Yes! I'd broken down and—*

She went to move, sit up, but couldn't. It was like she was pinned down. She was tied—no, chained—to a bed: a thin, stinking mattress beneath her, wire spring coils needling into her back. Instinctively, she tried touching her face but couldn't. Something held her arm back. Enraged, she began thrashing about, kicking her legs and pulling forward with her arms, like she was having some kind of fit. The metal bed frame bowed and bucked, joints creaked, but it was no good. She was held firmly in place.

"Motherfucker!" she screamed. "Let me fucking go!" Only after every ounce of energy was spent did she stop, ease back down, and take stock of her situation.

Just breathe. Stay calm.

Her wrists and ankles ached from the exertion, and her head was pounding, a splintering pain that bounced off the inside of her skull.

She felt like a puppet, limbs strung up. As far as she could tell, nothing seemed broken or overtly painful. Just her head and her wrists rubbed raw by the metal clamps and chains.

Was she in a hospital? A mental asylum? Is that why she was chained to a bed? *No. Talk sense, Emma.* It was the old man. He'd kidnapped her. But why? And why had he chained her to a bed? Like cold cement being poured slowly over her, dread crept along her body.

Now she realized why.

He was going to kill her. But only after he had done things, *unspeakable* things to her. It was all now making sense. Why else was she here like this?

She'd seen movies, horror movies, slasher flicks, was a big fan of them, too, until now. Women being abducted, then waking up chained in a barn or cabin or cave by some psychopath wearing a hockey mask or rubber Halloween hood, who was going to torture, then kill the girl. It was always a girl.

Stay calm. Stay calm.

She opened her eyes, thin, gritty slits at first, then blinked hard. The room came into focus, the ceiling, that is. Flat cement, spidery with cracks. A solitary light bulb dangling from a wire. Twisting her neck, she looked around some more, pulling her arms and legs together as far as the chains would allow. Thick, heavy clamps were snapped around each ankle and wrist and held her splayed to the corners of an old iron bed frame by the chain. *Thank God I still have my clothes on!* The air was chilly and had a dusty, damp tinge to it.

Looking past her feet was a door, heavy metal, lined with rivets or bolts, like an old prison cell door. There was a letterbox opening with a hatch set at eye level, the kind that slides back to reveal your jailer's creepy eyes. But the hatch was slid shut.

The entire room was like a chamber, bigger than a prison cell, she guessed.

Straining her neck and spine, Emma tilted her head up some

more. The floor was a slab of rough cement, stained in places with oil or grease and something else she couldn't tell, a muddy-brown color.

Emma craned her neck to her left and saw the large metal toolbox on the floor next to the wall, its cantilever trays unfurled up and outward, strange tools, pliers, lots of tools for pulling and cutting things, inside. She thrashed around again, refusing to cry, to beg. "Motherfu—"

The hatch in the door slid back with a grating noise, and two dark, soulless eyes peered at her.

Emma stopped thrashing and glared at the dark eyes. "You gutless fucker!" she snarled, spittle flying from her clenched teeth. "Unchain me, and let's see how brave you really are."

The eyes narrowed, like they were assessing her.

"That's right, you psycho fuck!" Emma yelled, pulling on her restraints. She didn't care. She wasn't about to crumble, curl up into some crying, sniveling ball and plead for her life. The only way out of here was to fight, to escape. She knew she was going to die one day. But not today. "You're a fucking coward hiding behind that door! You must have no dick and really tiny balls!"

The eyes dulled a fraction and turned colder.

Emma nodded. "Yeah, that's right, you dirty old fuck. You're not man enough, are you? You snatch women, then chain them up." With what saliva she had left in her dry mouth, she coughed up a ball of phlegm and spat out toward the door. "You pathetic dickless cun—"

The door suddenly swung back and clanged hard against the wall. Emma's next insult shrank back into her mouth before she could hurl it at the person who had just entered the room.

No! It made no sense. It can't...can't be...

Emma stared at the person, her mind doing backflips.

It's not possible. What kind of nightmare is this?

8

BV

The picture attached to the text message is of a young woman with blonde, shoulder-length hair, blue-gray eyes, pale skin, and she's staring defiantly down the camera lens, with not quite a sneer across her lips but very close.

She has a hard look in her eyes, like life keeps beating her down, but she doesn't care. She just keeps swinging—and according to the other information attached, she did just that. Put her fist into some poor guy's face. Broke his nose when he grabbed her on the ass in a coffee shop.

I like her already, yet my heart breaks thinking that she could be another victim, not just of Sam Pritchard, but of the thousands of predators out there trolling the highways, towns, and cities. She's wearing no makeup, either, doesn't need to. She has natural, home-grown, American-girl good looks that I can see through the thickened skin of her troubled gaze, making her seem older than eighteen.

Emma Karen Block was charged with common assault, got off with community service. That makes me happy because she doesn't look like much from what I can tell from the photo. Certainly not a hardened criminal. The assault was her only charge, I note as I keep reading the information I've been sent.

Before I can shoot back a reply, my cell rings. "Beatriz, what else have you found?" I ask.

I don't have the resources I once had to search for women, potential victims that are of the same age, look, and from the same geographic location where I think Pritchard is hunting as he cuts his murderous way across the country. So, I hired a contractor from the dark web, a young woman, a computer hacker of sorts who specializes in finding people who don't want to be found. Pedophiles, sex offenders, or unique missing persons.

I pay her well to scour the internet for me, do much of the legwork, sifting through and curating police missing-persons reports, the latest news bulletins from online media platforms, and law enforcement databases she can backdoor into, matching the profile I gave her based on Pritchard's past victims and MO. At first, we tried finding Pritchard himself, but he was elusive, a ghost who left only a trail of dead women in his wake. So, my secret hacker suggested we follow the trail by anticipating the next victim almost in real-time, within twenty-four hours of when another goes missing who fits Pritchard's taste in the women he kills.

I know I'm breaking the law, but Pritchard doesn't follow the law either. So, I have no choice. I'm out of the FBI, but Beatriz Vega has got me back "inside" with her computer skills and has assured me her hacks can't be traced back to her. Vega also sent me the cell phone I'm using to communicate with her. A piece of tech she had built specifically for all her clients, so communication between them is always encrypted.

"It's perhaps nothing, or perhaps something," Vega says on the line. "I'm in the FBI database at the moment, and a flag has just come up for Emma Block."

Vega sends me multiple screenshots of what she's looking at right now on her computer screen. A missing-persons report was filed in Georgia twelve hours ago for Emma Block by her mother, Karen. For some reason, it was flagged by the FBI, and I think I know by whom:

Aaron Wood, my counterpart within the FBI. We are both chasing Pritchard, following a line of red pins on a map, west to east across America that Wood has on his office wall in Virginia. Each red pin denotes a crime scene where Pritchard has dumped a body. But it's historical, after the fact. Whereas Vega and I are trying to predict where he'll strike next, get ahead of the death curve, so to speak.

I study the photo again of Emma Block. Could she be next? Has Pritchard snatched her and is now holding her, or is she already dead, dumped by him in some shallow grave or deep inside some lonely cave?

I tell Beatriz to keep digging on this woman and let me know what else she finds. Then I ended the call.

No doubt Aaron Wood is working off his own profile the FBI worked up, based on past victimology. But I doubt they'd be trying to anticipate his next location based on recent, still-warm missing-persons data. Yet Emma Block was flagged by the FBI.

Grabbing a cup of coffee, I go to my room downstairs, flip on the lights, and look at the map on the wall. My pins are also red, but I've extended them with a series of green pins, likely towns Pritchard might pass through. I stand at the map, holding my phone up, comparing Emma Block to the others. She is similar to the other young women he likes to kidnap, torture, then kill.

But there's one problem. The location is wrong. My trajectory for Pritchard's route continues east. Emma Block went missing two hundred miles due south of that anticipated line.

Why? I ponder what I can't answer, for a few minutes, sipping my coffee that's now gone cold. Why would he deviate? Since he began, he's been moving steadily east. He should be out of Georgia and into South Carolina by now.

Maybe I'm reading too much into this. We've had no hits for a few months now. Maybe I want Emma Block to be his next victim rather than just a runaway or unrelated missing person.

I study the photo some more, almost willing the young woman to whisper to me it's her that Pritchard has taken. Could it be? I don't know. My thumb hovers over the delete button on my cell phone.

The geography doesn't align. Then I decide. Someone else may have taken her, or she'll turn up in a few days' time.

I press delete, then text Vega to stop any further research on Emma Block. It's a false lead.

9

LIES

My cell phone rings, and I look at the screen.

It's a number I'm familiar with, a caller I know, yet a flicker of dread rises within me. Does he know? Does he know that Beatriz Vega has hacked his computer system and that she's been rifling through his case files? Why else would he be calling? I've made my intentions very clear to him and Dan Miller, my ex-partner within the bureau.

I take the call.

"Carolyn, how are you?" Aaron Wood's cheerful voice vibrates in my ear.

"I'm fine, Aaron. What's up?" I say matter-of-factly. I haven't spoken to him in three months, and his phone call is unexpected or perhaps expected in a bad way. He's not calling to shoot the breeze or talk about how the Orioles are doing during spring training in his home state of Maryland. That's not Aaron. Everything he does is with purpose and only after careful consideration.

"Nothing," Aaron says a little too breezily. "I'm just checking in on you. See how you're feeling. It's been a while since we last chatted."

He doesn't do "chatting" either. Does he know and wants me to admit to it?

"How are you coping? Fully recuperated?"

Coping? Recuperated? The words rile me, make me feel like a decrepit, old person convalescing in a nursing home in Boca Raton. "I'm coping just fine." My mind flits back to the frayed piece of coarse rope dangling from the gnarly cypress tree. "I'm doing well. Almost fully recovered." That part is the truth. I push aside the bad images in my head of me standing under that lone cypress with a noose around my neck. Not because I want to, but because I must. I need to remain focused.

There's an awkward pause in the conversation. He wants to ask me something. I can feel it in the airwaves between us.

"I spoke to Dan again this morning." Aaron finally breaks the silence.

I swallow an almost audible sigh of relief. He doesn't know we've hacked into his computer files.

"He mentioned you again, Carolyn. He wants to know if I can try to persuade you again to come back."

"We've already discussed this, Aaron. I'm not coming back."

"I know, Carolyn. It's just that—"

I cut him off before he finishes. "You don't need me, Aaron. You can find Pritchard all on your own. I'm out. I need to do other things."

"You're not searching for Pritchard on your own?"

The directness of his question takes me by surprise. "Is this why you're calling me?"

"I thought you might consider it."

"I wouldn't know where to start, Aaron. Plus, I don't have the resources I once had when I was working for the FBI." I think of Vega. From what I've seen of her so far, she'd run rings around anyone inside the FBI.

"Good," he says. "I thought I'd just ask, anyway."

I've had this same conversation many times before, and he knows my feelings about it.

While I loved my time with the FBI, if I'm going to catch Sam

Pritchard, I need to do it on my own terms. The FBI has almost unlimited resources and a massive budget. But it's too slow, cumbersome, filled with political bureaucracy, endless box-ticking and pointless rules. I'm faster on my own, nimbler. Sam Pritchard will see the FBI coming a mile away. He did before and we lost him. He escaped again despite a team of elite HRT members surrounding him in a cave system in Nevada.

"Give my regards to Dan," I tell Aaron. "We'll catch up sometime, have a beer, reminisce about the good ol' days." As I say it, I know it's never going to happen. The path I've chosen, there's no coming back from. It's a one-way ticket, with Pritchard waiting for me at the other end.

"If you go after Pritchard on your own," Aaron continues, "he will kill you this time, Carolyn."

My answer seems not to have convinced Aaron. He knows me all too well. We were a good team—once. My impatience and dislike for following the rules in the field complemented his sage-but-pragmatic advice and brilliant forensic mind in the FBI labs.

We are all going to die, eventually, I want to say, but I don't. "I found Robin Hood on my own, and caught him too." With immense help from a dear friend, who also saved my life, I might add.

"And look where that got you," Aaron retorts. "You almost died."

The comment makes me angry. "Look, Aaron," I say. "I'm not interested in Sam Pritchard. I don't know why you think I'm going on some personal crusade to catch him." I have no trouble lying to Aaron about this. I'll do whatever it takes to find Pritchard. Burn bridges, trash friendships, even break the law, which I'm now doing with Vega. I don't care. I stopped caring long ago. The only thing that's keeping me alive is the need to find Pritchard before he kills any more women.

Aaron's comeback is quick and has some truth in it. "Because I know you better than anyone else, Carolyn."

I pause for a moment. Well, there are certain things about me right now that you do not know about.

He continues. "And I know you can be a vindictive and vengeful kind of person."

I smile. Yes. I can be.

"Don't become like him, just to catch him," Aaron warns.

That's good advice for someone other than me because it's bullshit. If I'm going to catch Pritchard, then I must think like him. Be like him—obviously not kill anyone. But I need to crawl inside his demented head, look at the world through his warped lens, and figure out where he's going to strike next. "I'm fine, Aaron," I reply. "I need to sort out some personal matters now. That's my priority." More lies. Aaron doesn't know about Vega hacking into the FBI system, otherwise he would mention it straight up. He's just fishing, curious to know if I'm hunting Pritchard myself.

I end the call, telling Aaron that we'll catch up soon.

I stare at the women on the wall, wondering if I can catch Pritchard on my own. I don't have the massive resources behind me I once had. I'm an outsider now, a loner.

And that fact makes me even more determined.

10

MISSING

In his mid-thirties, Aaron Wood had owlish features, dark floppy hair, which he constantly had to sweep from his eyes, long limbs, and hands like a world-class pianist, long and delicate, able to forage, poke, and search the narrowest of crevices, thinnest of cracks, and the deepest of spaces in his relentless quest for forensic evidence.

His colleagues often said that to watch Wood at his desk on his computer keyboard was to watch Johann Sebastian Bach belt out a feverish rendition of his famous Piano Partita No. 2 in C Minor. At times, Wood appeared to make love to the computer keys. Other times, it was like each individual key was responsible for every childhood failure he had ever suffered. Slightly goofy, plenty smart, truly gifted, and resembling a mad scientist, Wood, during his short tenure with the FBI, had tracked down more serial killers than anyone else in the bureau's history.

Apart from his job, Wood only had two other addictions: Death Wish coffee, the highest caffeine coffee commercially available, and caffeine-rich energy drinks that he kept in a fully stocked mini fridge under his desk in his office. It was a dangerous combination and probably the main reason he slept so little.

He detested social media in all its forms and only had a cell phone at the behest of the bureau so he could be reached all hours of the day and night.

When not working a crime scene, Wood was either ensconced in the comfort and familiarity of his corner office or seen roaming restlessly within the FBI labs in Virginia during the darkest hours before dawn, when, accordingly to him, the most murderous of serial killers were also awake stalking their prey. For hours on end, he would be perched on a lab stool, staring relentlessly at bone fragments or pieces of a skull, or items of torn and bloodied clothing, trying to build a mental trail of a victim's last movements in reverse that would lead him and a team of agents back to where the perpetrator first made contact with their intended target.

Wood's large, peering hazel eyes were magnified by the thick, black-framed spectacles he wore, making him look like Brains from *Thunderbirds* as he stared at his cell phone as it lay on his desk, his brow furrowed, the call with Carolyn Ryder having just ended. Wood prided himself on his intuition, and at this moment, it was telling him that Ryder wasn't being completely honest with him. Was she hunting Pritchard? Despite Ryder's words of reassurance, he wasn't entirely convinced that she wasn't. There was just something in her voice, masking a truth that seemed hidden.

He knew Ryder wasn't one to rest on her laurels, and she had a vengeful streak. Several times he had witnessed her firsthand beating a perpetrator with her fists before tactical agents could pull her off.

While on a case, Ryder had relentless focus, often going days without eating or sleeping or even showering. And she would hound him all hours, always wanting to know what else he could tell her about the latest and worst monster they were hunting. Always wanting to be first through the door to make an arrest or to save an already dead victim. That was when she took it upon herself to dish out some of her own justice. She had been one of the rising stars who, in the pursuit of catching some of the worst serial murderers, had maybe burned a little too bright for her own good. Yet, in Wood's opinion, she lacked the lofty ego that typically went hand in hand with such a meteoric rise within such a male-dominated organization.

Ryder was technically dead when they hauled her near-frozen body onto the operating table, after Robin Hood, the notorious Midwestern winter serial killer, had shot her with his crossbow. And this was after she had resigned from the FBI and had returned to Willow Falls, Iowa, to bury her mother, who had died from a long illness.

Ryder had survived but had changed. She had become more insular, withdrawn, dark, and brooding. Sure, that was expected. She had cheated death at the hands of Sam Pritchard, too. The cumulative effect was bound to impact her mental and physical state. Yet she refused counseling from an FBI shrink.

They were a great team, her and Wood, while it lasted. Wood put all his forensic skills and tools into tracking down the monsters, guiding Ryder in the field, then Ryder would go in for the kill and apprehend them.

Wood glanced at the map on his wall, at the line of red pins snaking west to east, Sam Pritchard's bloody footprints. Was Ryder also following the same footprints? Perhaps. But how? She was alone, was a civilian now, with civilian resources. She certainly didn't have access to any of the shock and awe and reach the FBI did across all law enforcement jurisdictions that Wood had at his fingertips.

Moving his computer mouse, Wood refocused on the file he had been sent. A young woman who had gone missing. Emma Block. He spent the next few minutes reading the file before closing it, convinced that Emma Block was an ordinary missing-persons case. The location where the young woman had gone missing was too far south for Wood's liking. Pritchard tended to move in straight lines along highways due to the fact that he was a long-distance truck driver.

After taking a swig of his now-cold coffee, Wood then sent the file back, unflagging the missing eighteen-year-old as a potential next victim of Pritchard, thereby kicking it back to local law enforcement for them to handle. Pretty, with blonde, shoulder-length hair and fresh, youthful features, despite the rebellious sneer, she certainly fit alongside the other young women Pritchard had killed. But that wasn't enough for Wood. Emma Block, unfortunately, was just one of many who went missing each year across this big, wide land. Maybe she would turn up, or maybe she had been taken by someone else.

But for the moment, Wood was resigned to the fact that Emma Block didn't warrant his special attention.

11

AN UGLY TWIST

An old woman stood in the doorway. Wide-hipped and overweight, she had pallid skin and a greasy, soiled look to her with a cruel, unforgiving sparkle in her dark, beady eyes.

She regarded Emma as a child might after unwrapping a gift from Santa, who had rolled everything she could ever wish for into one massive present.

Ignoring the sudden tightening of her throat, Emma raised her chin and glared defiantly back at the old woman. Being still chained to the bed, that was the limit of all she could do—that and hurl abuse. "Fucking bitch, let me go!" Emma pulled on the chains, and the bed rattled and rocked in creaking protest.

As though she were deaf, the abuse seemed to deflect off the woman, like she had heard it all many times before and was immune.

She seemed about the same age as Emma's grandmother, sixty-five, but with a more weathered, more hardened look that spoke of a different kind of life experience. Her gray hair seemed dead, had the look of brittle sun-bleached seaweed that had washed up on the shore. With a thick torso, and chubby legs that protruded from under a bland skirt, she was compact, squat, and clad in a billowing, sweat-stained shirt that couldn't hide the plentiful rolls of fat underneath.

However, the most disturbing feature of all that caught Emma's attention after she stopped thrashing around on the rickety bed was a thick, silvery scar that cut away from one corner of the old woman's mouth. A grotesque past injury, no doubt, as though a large fishing hook had been caught in her mouth, then ripped sideways, splitting the skin outward along the cheek only to then be sewn up with crude, exaggerated stitches. It elongated one side of her mouth into the Joker's heinous, comical grin.

The woman stepped forward, then tossed a plastic water bottle at Emma. It landed expertly between her legs as though intentionally aimed.

Emma grimaced and twisted her head, forcing down a cry of pain that rose in her throat, not wanting to give the old bitch the satisfaction. Emma's nostrils flared as she billowed like a galloping racehorse at the woman, rage seething behind her pursed lips. With her hands chained, how the hell was she supposed to drink the water?

The woman's mouth twisted in a cruel sneer, and she nodded with apparent satisfaction.

Emma flinched as the woman produced a knife, then came forward and sat next to her, the bed almost collapsing under her weight. She pressed the knife under Emma's left breast, then paused.

Grinding her teeth, Emma watched as the tip of the blade slowly traced the outline of her breast, before coming to rest on top where her nipple lay under the thin fabric of her crop top. The woman cocked her head, her gaze transfixed on the sharp point of the knife as she then began to tease the nipple erect through the fabric. "So pretty," she muttered, her voice like gravel. "So young. So soft." She looked up at Emma. "It would be such a pity if I have to remove one of these." Her grotesque smile widened some more. "Both, even." Her thick tongue rolled over her teeth as she pushed the tip of the blade into Emma's breast. "Such a pity it would be."

Under the downward pressure of the knife, Emma could feel the material of her clothing on the verge of splitting open. Tears filled her eyes, but she refused to cry out. Her breath came in shallow gasps for fear that any pronounced upward movement of her chest would cause the blade to sink through the material and puncture her skin.

The woman tilted her head up and peered down at her. "Good," she said, licking her lips, a slovenly look in her eyes. "You learn fast." With her other hand, she withdrew a key and unlocked both wrist manacles and one ankle manacle while the knife remained pressed firmly into Emma's breast. One leg was still chained to the bed, and that section of chain had been wrapped several times around the top of the bed post. Now with both her wrists and one foot free, she was more mobile and could unravel the chain from the top of the post even though it was still tethering her to the bed. However, Emma remained lying where she was, her arms raised above her head.

The woman eased back, then got off the bed.

With her thirst raging, Emma looked down longingly at the plastic bottle that was now within reach. But she refused to grab the bottle and gobble down the water. Giving in and showing weakness wasn't part of the game she wanted to play. And for her, and for pigs like this woman, it was a game, using fear to break down a person's resolve.

No. Despite what she had just endured, Emma wasn't going to give the ugly, deformed bitch the pleasure.

And there was no food despite Emma being hungry. Just water. This concerned her. Were they going to feed her? If not, that could only mean one thing: they intended to make her weak. She would be less resistant, less likely to fight back effectively. But Emma had other plans.

Also, the woman's face wasn't covered. Not a good sign either. They intended to kill her—eventually.

"My name is Dolores," the woman said, eyeing Emma almost in a new light. "But you can call me, Dolly."

Dolly? Emma pivoted and sat up on the mattress, ignoring the water bottle. *As if the fuck I'm gonna call you that, bitch.* And where was the old man who had kidnapped her in the first place? Were they a tag team? The two of them abducting people? Her father would have called the police by now, her mother maybe not so fast. And surely her car, abandoned on the side of the road with the hood up, would have been discovered, too.

Emma rubbed her wrists from where the steel manacles had chaffed the skin red-raw.

"Em-ma Ka-ren Bloc-k," the woman said, her thick tongue lavish and slippery on each syllable of her name, as though she were salivating, leaving no doubt in Emma's mind what her intentions were.

Emma glared at her but kept quiet. They must have taken her purse where her driver's license was stored. Her duffel bag and cell phone, too. Thankfully, her cell was locked with a pass code.

"If you comply," the woman continued, her eyes crawling slowly over Emma's body, "then we will let you go."

Emma choked down a laugh. *Yeah. Fat chance there, Freddy.* And the old man was there, too, somewhere. The woman had said "we."

"*If* you comply," the woman repeated.

Comply with what? She was going to die. That much Emma knew if she didn't get out of this hellhole. Yet what worried her the most was what the woman was going to do to her, and for how long, before she got the chance to escape.

12

I HAVE YOU

Beatriz Vega couldn't sleep. Something wouldn't let her, which was unusual.

Despite her line of work, she usually slept soundly at night, cocooned in her converted warehouse fortress in a desolate, industrial part of New York City where she ate, slept, lived, and hunted those just like her: people who didn't want to be found.

The thirty-one-year-old, a native of Lima, Peru was short in stature but towering with presence: coal-black hair, olive skin, and impatient brown eyes, with a brain that she could switch on and off when needed. That was how she had remained sane for all these years. But it was the last call she'd had with Carolyn Ryder that was troubling her enough now to roll out of bed and check her watch.

Two a.m.

Vega made her way to a large open-plan kitchen. The cavernous interior of the warehouse, designed by her, mirrored her own personality: bare concrete walls with exposed brickwork, overhead sprinkler pipes, ventilation ductwork, sheet metal, rust-stained girders, lashings of rivets and bolts, and bare wood-plank floors. *Architectural Digest* would term it "industrial chic meets high-end technology." Set amid a camouflage of shadowy grays, blacks, and charcoals, the design and layout were practical and unpretentious. Tall glass windows framed in thin black steel ran the entire length of one side of the warehouse. A long custom-made desk, made from repurposed wood, salvaged from an abandoned wharf, stood against the windows with a solitary flat-panel display taking pride of place sitting at its center, the screen a messy maze of scrolling text, symbols, and numbers.

The stainless-steel commercial espresso machine hissed and spat as she worked the knobs and ground coffee beans before extracting a velvety smooth shot of espresso into a shot glass.

When Beatriz Vega was just a precocious twelve-year-old, she caught the attention of her mathematics schoolteacher as a gifted, intelligent child, with an acute ability to create complex algorithms and data structures to rival the skills of the best university professors. When she turned sixteen, a representative of Peru's National Directorate of Intelligence paid her parents a visit and offered Beatriz a fast-track career path in their cyber protection division. After ten years of working for the Peruvian government, including a stint with the military, Vega left and struck out on her own.

Now she was a freelancer, with a select group of legitimate private clients, and despite her sometimes fiery Peruvian blood and proud heritage, Vega had refused all subsequent governmental approaches for her services. She didn't hate governments, but a ten-year career of working for one had left Vega with a healthy distrust of them—all of them. She now preferred to put her unique skills toward more altruistic endeavors, like tracking down global pedophile rings and sex-trafficking networks on behalf of international charities and interest groups who lacked the daunting resources, capabilities, and stealthy reach Vega had gained over the years.

But money talks. It loosens lips, points fingers, and provides names and addresses—both digital and physical—of where evil hides and masquerades as decent, honest citizens.

So, the money to finance Vega's operation came courtesy of her secretly wading, bucket in hand, into the virtual river of digital money that flowed illegally into the offshore bank accounts of various tax havens around the world. In her mind, she was taxing the tax cheats and repurposing the money for more humanitarian purposes. It had also allowed Vega to "vanish" off the face of the earth, purchase the disused building, and convert it into a fortress where she now lived.

Espresso in hand, she went to her desk and called up the map location of where Emma Block's car was found abandoned. For several minutes, she stared at the satellite location while sipping her espresso. While Ryder may have dismissed Emma Block as a potential victim of Sam Pritchard, Vega was less reluctant. Something was niggling at her. And from her wealth of experience, such a niggle usually meant she needed to dig a little further, peel back a few more layers and see who was hiding beneath. While we're all creatures of habit, Vega knew cunning people changed their habits because they knew they were being tracked.

Were they looking at this all wrong?

Despite their best efforts, Ryder and Vega had not one solid, fresh lead on Pritchard. It was as though he'd vanished into thin air, since his last victim, a girl whose body he had dumped in some dark, damp cave. They had been searching for a rendition of Pritchard with some minor changes. Maybe he wasn't a long-haul truck driver anymore. Maybe he was driving a simple sedan. No, that wouldn't make sense, Vega thought as she continued staring at the map on the screen.

He needed to transport his victims. Maybe a pickup truck? Vega needed to look at this from a different angle, an alternate perspective. They were searching for what Pritchard had been driving and how he had looked.

With a flick of the computer mouse, she zoomed out the map location to a twenty-mile radius to reveal a circular patchwork quilt of green, pivot-irrigated fields so common in the Midwest and southern states.

Then something in the upper left corner caught her eye. She immediately zoomed in on the small structure.

A gas station.

She began circling it with her cursor pointer while thinking. *Maybe?*

The only other structures were ten miles farther to the west, in a small community by the looks of it, with a motel and a small strip of stores. Perhaps that was where Emma was heading, to meet with her father, as per the brief police report Vega had lifted from the police database.

It took Vega only ten minutes to find the company that owned the remote gas station in question, then another ten minutes to hack into their online cloud security-camera backup system. Next, she chose two cameras that gave a clear view in both directions of the forecourt where the gas pumps were located. After setting an initial search time frame of twenty-four hours on either side of the approximate time Emma Block had—according to her mother, Karen—left home, Vega then kicked on her facial-recognition software. A swarm of small green squares appeared on the computer screen, then rapidly jumped from face to face of the gas station customers as the video footage was played at speed, capturing the images of the drivers as they exited their vehicles to fill up at the pump, then walking to and from the convenience store. Vega sat and watched as the software searched out a facial match between customers and the facial topography map she had built from several photos of Pritchard, including his DMV photo and heavy-haulage license.

After yawning and then draining her third espresso, Vega went back to bed, allowing the computer to churn through the video footage.

Back under the thick comforter, the niggling sensation had abated in Vega's head, for the time being, and she slept soundly for two hours, until her cell phone pinged.

She bolted upright in bed and pulled her cell phone to her face.

There was a match.

Vega literally ran to her computer and jumped into the chair, the edges of her lips tingling. This was how she got when she'd made a much-needed breakthrough in finding a missing person.

Staring at the computer screen, icy water was thrown on her initial excitement.

Seventy percent.

It was a seventy percent match. Well below the acceptable threshold set for all her searches.

Shaking off the disappointment, she enhanced the image. It was of an older male who owned a large, dark pickup, possibly a RAM or Ford Super Duty. The software had made a composite of several images taken of him standing by the gas pump while filling up, then walking back from the store after grabbing a coffee.

Vega captured the license plates on the truck, then ran them through the DMV and came back with a much clearer picture of him and his details.

Walter Bickford. The address was probably some mailbox nailed to a tree along some desolate dirt track in the middle of nowhere. Calling up maps again, Vega confirmed her hypothesis.

Comparing the images side by side—the actual DMV mugshot-style photo of Walter Bickford with the facial topography map Vega had constructed of Pritchard—the software then came back with an eighty-six percent match.

Better.

Still well below her parameter of ninety-five percent but getting closer.

Next, she compared the images visually, allowing her gut instinct —something a computer program could not mimic—to decide for her. While the software she had designed and coded did allow for alterations in physical appearance such as aging, change of hair color, weight fluctuations, and even plastic surgery, nothing could beat good old-fashioned female intuition.

Vega stared at the screen. The tingling around her lips had now spread to her cheeks and jaw. She muttered something uncomplimentary in Aymara—a native language also spoken in Peru—rather than Spanish. She leaned in closer to the screen and smiled. "Motherfucker," she whispered. "I have you."

Grabbing her cell phone, she called Ryder, who answered after two rings, groggy with sleep. "Yep."

"Carolyn, I've found him. And I think he *has* taken Emma Block."

13

FIGHTING CHANCE

The woman who answers the door has the same beaten-down look in her eyes I saw etched in the face of Emma Block, which glared out at me from the photos Vega had sent me two days ago—just older.

She's thirty-six, yet a few loose strands of premature gray blow in the spring heat around her face, which is lined with years of hard work and little reward, making her age look more like in her fifties. But she still cares about her daughter. I can see a glimmer of hope there, deep in her eyes.

I had flown into Columbus, Georgia, picked up a rental car, then drove two hours south to the city of Camilla, in Mitchell County where Karen Block, Emma Block's mother lives. Camilla, with a population of around seven thousand, was the historical site of a massacre of black protesters in 1868 by white townsfolk, who opened fire upon participants in an organized rally who were protesting for political and social reform.

"Mrs. Block?" I ask.

Karen Block lets out a sigh. "It's about time," she scoffs before unlocking the screen door. "I called you guys again, and still no one has called me back. Now you decide to show up?"

Before I can answer, she opens the door, and I see an opportunity buried in apparent confusion. Quickly, I step inside and follow her into the gloomy interior of the trailer park duplex. Down a small hallway and into a living room arranged with worn furniture, I go. Karen may not have much, but I can see she makes the best of what she has. The room is pleasant, clean, and an old boxy television flickers on a stand in one corner, while six pairs of gray eyes scrutinize me from a laminate side table: photos of Emma during the various stages of her young and hopefully not short life.

Karen Block slumps into a rumpled sofa covered with throw rugs, then looks up at me. "I need my car back," she says. "I can't have it impounded. I've been off work for days now, and I've got bills to pay."

She doesn't think her daughter, her only child, who has been missing for two days now, is actually missing.

When I don't answer, she looks at me suspiciously. "You don't look like a sheriff's deputy."

That's because I'm not. I gave up long ago wondering when I first started breaking the law, so I continue to play along with the charade. It may be my only hope of getting any useful information out of the mother of the daughter who Vega thinks was snatched by Pritchard.

Karen Block waves a hand in the air. "I called three times, and I thought they'd send someone out sooner."

Doubling down on the lie, I take out a notebook. "I'm sorry, Mrs. Block. I'd like to ask you some questions about Emma."

"She took off to see her worthless father!" she sneers. "I told her not to, but she took my car keys and went anyway." She looks away, her mouth curled in distaste. "He's a useless bum." She glances back at me. "My car must've broken down, and he probably picked her up. That, or she hitched a ride with one of her ex-boyfriends."

"One of her ex-boyfriends?" I ask. "Who would that—"

"Don't get me wrong," Karen interrupts me. "My daughter doesn't sleep around. She just has a lot of male friends. Good people."

"Have you tried calling any of them?" I ask.

Karen shakes her head. "I tried calling Emma's cell. But it doesn't connect."

That is a concern.

"And does she do this at times? Go missing for days?"

"A few times. Usually when she's angry with the world or just wants her space. Then she turns up a few days later, acting as though nothing has happened. That's why I'm not too worried this time. I just want my car back."

So, the glimmer of hope I saw before was about the car, not Emma. "Aren't you concerned about why your car was found abandoned? Isn't that why you called the sheriff's department and filed a missing-persons report?"

Karen gives a shrug. "I thought I'd teach her a lesson this time. Leave it to the police to find her. Maybe she'll think twice again about disappearing with my car when the police catch up with her. That's why I rang again. But they sent no one to see me. Now you show up today."

"What's the longest Emma has gone missing before, without being in contact with you?"

"A week perhaps."

A week. If Vega is right, and Pritchard has her, Emma Block will be dead within the week and left as carrion.

"Look, it's probably nothing," Karen continues. "She'll call in a few days' time. I'm just angry she left the car like how she did."

Why would an eighteen-year-old young girl leave a car abandoned on the side of the road, then vanish without a good reason? It makes little sense to me. Mother and daughter seem independent, and they might expect this kind of behavior between them. Seems like the sheriff's department doesn't really care, either, as it sounds like Emma has a history of disappearing for a few days.

"Have you tried contacting your ex-husband to see if Emma is with him?"

My question almost chokes her. "I'm not calling that useless bum.

He walked out on both of our lives when Emma was just a baby, and now he shows up, wanting us to be all one big happy family again?"

I glance over at the photos of Emma, then turn back to Karen. "So, what can you tell me about Emma? What is she like?"

Karen shrugs. "Just a normal teenager. But she's a fighter."

"A fighter?"

Karen gives a proud nod before getting up, then disappearing into another room, only to return moments later with another photo frame in her hand, which she gives to me.

It's a photo of Emma with a young woman, arms around each other's shoulders, big smiles, and bright eyes. I recognize the other woman in the picture. Many probably wouldn't. I look up at Karen Block. "Is this...?"

She nods. "Ronda Rousey. She's Emma's hero. Always has been since she was a little girl. She's the reason she took up mixed martial arts."

"Emma took up MMA?"

Karen nods again. "That's why I'm not too worried this time about her going missing and all. She can take care of herself." The sofa creaks in protest as Karen slumps back down again. She points at the photo in my hand. "She met Ronda a few years back at a UFC event. Said it was the best day of her life. She wanted to be just like Ronda. A strong, kick-ass woman." Karen smiles for the first time. "Emma has always been a tomboy. Always getting into fights with boys ever since she was in school. That's how she is. A youth counselor suggested it would be good for her to maybe take out her aggression in martial arts. So, one day she saw Ronda Rousey take down some woman twice her size in a tournament and got inspired. The next day, she signed right up for karate and Jujitsu lessons. Paid for it all herself with a part-time job she'd gotten at the local dollar store."

This is interesting. I add it to my notes and wonder how many of Pritchard's other victims also thought they could look after themselves.

Karen gets up again and goes to the sideboard, opens up the compartment and comes back with a trophy and hands it to me. There is a gold figurine on it, throwing a karate kick. I read the small plaque on the trophy and my heart stutters. I look up at Karen, and she is looking down at me, a wider smile on her face now. "National All Styles Champion for her age group. Three years in a row. Like I said. She is more than capable of looking after herself."

I look at the trophy in my hand. But is she capable of fighting off someone like Sam Pritchard, the Highway Killer, who has abducted and murdered more than twenty women?

14

THE TEST

After Dolly had left, Emma gulped down the entire contents of the water bottle.

It was enough to quench her thirst for the moment.

Using her hands, she unraveled the chain from around the top of the bed post and stood. She had about three feet of chain now, enough slack for her to take a few steps before the chain went taut, holding her ankle back. Her eyes settled on the metal toolbox that was sitting open on the floor beyond her reach. The heavy metal door was locked, and the sliding viewing hatch was closed, so she felt alone, that no one could see her. Maybe she could drag the bed all the way to the toolbox? It must be only seven or eight feet away. Surely there would be something inside she could use to cut the chain around her ankle or she could use as a weapon.

Emma didn't move, her eyes remained focused on the red metal toolbox. It seemed so agonizingly close, a glittering lure that was now the center of her entire universe. Her eyes darted to the heavy metal door as an unsettling thought crept into her head. Was it a test? A trap even? Who left an open toolbox within reach of someone who was chained up? Emma bit her lip, indecision slowly seeping into her as she looked back at the toolbox. It seemed too obvious. Were they watching her right now? Seeing what she would do? She suddenly felt like a rat in a cage being tempted by a piece of cheese or a chimpanzee with a banana dangling in front of them.

Looking around the room, she could see no obvious security cameras. Then again, as she had seen on television documentaries, nanny cams could be the size of a thumbnail and could be hidden anywhere. Apart from the bed and the toolbox, the room was empty —wasn't it?

Where could a camera be hidden?

Emma tugged at the chain. There was no way she was going to break it with her bare hands. The links were too thick, heavy steel, and the joints solidly welded, by the looks of them. She needed something like a metal saw to cut through the links, and maybe there was one in the toolbox.

If you comply, then we will let you go. The words Dolores or Dolly, or whatever the fuck her name was, echoed inside Emma's head. That was what the woman had said. But what did she mean? *Comply?* Comply to what? The perverted old witch hadn't elaborated.

She looked down at a tattoo on the inside of her forearm, a skull between an hourglass and a wilting flower in a vase. *Remember, you must die.* It was a constant reminder of how precious life was and not to waste a single second of it. And she was determined not to die today, and certainly not at the hands of these two monsters. Where was the old man, anyway? Obviously, they were a tag team.

Wrapping both her hands around the bed frame, Emma knew one thing for certain. She was going to die in this hellhole if she did nothing.

Inch by screeching inch, she began dragging the bed she was chained to across the rough cement floor.

As she heaved the bed, a thought entered her head. Maybe they were going to rape her first, before killing her? The old woman certainly seemed keen to get her hands on Emma, the way she wielded that knife.

A recent memory forced its way into Emma's mind, and she pictured another gloomy room, not unlike the one she was now in. It was a basement under a house, loud thumping music coming through the ceiling above. The room had been dimly lit, crammed with old boxes and discarded furniture. A boiler sat hunkered in the corner next to a washing machine and dryer combo. The room smelled musty, of damp and rotting things. Emma remembered it like it was just yesterday as she descended the stairs, looking for her friend Kate. It was Kate's idea to come to the party. Emma hadn't wanted to go. It was the usual high school crowd of familiar, drunk, and doped-out, faces. Guys with their shirts off, playing stupid drinking games. Girls in dark corners being enticed with pills. Within an hour of their arrival, Emma knew Kate had drunk too much too quickly and had drawn the leering gaze of a few guys as she danced carefree in the back-yard to the tunes of Taylor Swift. Then Kate had disappeared, and Emma went searching for her among the throng of people. That's what friends do, look out for each other, especially at parties where drugs, booze, and sleazy guys looking to score, were plentiful.

In the basement, Emma had found Kate lying on a tattered orange sofa covered in cat hair, the arms ripped, its inside stuffing spilling out like fatty tissue from an open wound. To Emma, Kate, with her skirt hoisted up around her waist and her panties dangling from one ankle, looked unconscious on the sofa. The guy on top of her—with his shorts down around his knees, his hips thrusting into her like a pile driver, grunting and groaning like a rutting pig—certainly wasn't. Emma's mind went numb, and a red haze descended over her eyes. She knew the guy, and she also knew that Kate wouldn't have agreed to this and had rebuked him plenty of times before. It was obvious the guy had taken full advantage of Kate, had isolated her from Emma during the party, then lured her into the basement to force himself on her.

Wrenching him off Kate's listless body, Emma hit him several times in the face with her fist and kept hitting him until he collapsed into a bloody heap on the floor.

After some coaxing and a few slaps to the face, Emma managed to get Kate to a semiconscious state where she helped her friend out of the basement. After rushing to her own home, they crept into the house together while Emma's mother was still asleep, and she sat Kate in the shower and scrubbed her skin raw until the hot water turned cold. On the way home, she had asked the Uber driver to stop off at a drugstore where she went in and bought the morning-after pill for her friend, just to make sure.

Going to the police would be pointless because it would be his word versus Kate and Emma's: *Oh, no, Officer,* he would say, Emma imagined. *She definitely wanted it.* And *Yes, sir, she initiated it, not me. She came willingly down to the dirty, roach-infested basement to have my cock thrust into both her openings.*

Yes. It was only when Kate called Emma the next day in tears after she had sat on the toilet did she discover that little dirty secret.

Emma's only regret was that she wished she could have saved her friend before the whole sordid deed had happened.

Emma pulled harder on the bed, dragging it some more. She would kill the person who tried to touch her like that.

15

PAIN NOT PLEASURE

Emma continued pulling the bed toward the toolbox.

The frame was heavy old steel, not new aluminum, yet it was rickety like she was pulling a pile of loose junk metal. A few bolts holding some of the brackets had sheared off, making Emma wonder how many others just like her had occupied that same bed and what their fate had been.

Inch by inch, she dragged the bed, until finally the toolbox was within reach. She took precious minutes to search through the contents. Pliers, alligator clips, a hammer. She held the hammer in one hand and gave it a few practice swings, thinking of Bruce Willis in *Pulp Fiction*. Pity there was no chainsaw or samurai sword lying around. The thought of smashing the claw of the hammer down on the old witch's skull, cracking it open like an ostrich egg, and watching all the gray pus ooze out brought a smile to Emma's face.

But how could she hide the hammer? The old witch would get suspicious if she saw that Emma was hiding something behind her back. Maybe under the mattress? Yeah. That would work. Wait until she got close enough, then wham!

To Emma's dismay, there were no knives or a saw that she could use to cut through the chain. There was something that looked like sharp pliers, tin snips maybe. She tried cutting a link with them, but the jaws were too narrow and didn't even leave a mark on the surface.

She glanced up. Was that a sound she'd heard from the other side of the heavy metal door? Like keys jangling?

Her heart beat harder.

If you comply.

Maybe it was nothing. Crouching down, she went back to searching the toolbox. Even if she found something to cut through the chain, what next? The door was heavy steel, like one of those prison doors she remembered seeing on a television documentary about Alcatraz. How would she get through it? She needed the key that the woman had.

Suddenly, the door behind her unlocked.

Emma whirled around, brandishing the tin snips in her hand.

The old witch stood in the doorway, her wide girth almost filling it completely. Immediately, her eyes cut to the tin snips in Emma's hand. "They won't cut through that chain, darling," she said, an evil twinkle bouncing off the dark orbs of her eyes. She stepped toward Emma. "But they'll cut through your pretty little finger bones and toes like cookie dough."

The threat was implicit. Emma glanced at the tin snips in her hand before tossing them back into the toolbox. *If you comply.*

There was something odd about the old woman that Emma noticed. It was how she was standing, with one hand behind her back.

Slowly, the woman withdrew her hand.

Emma's breath caught in her throat when she saw the thing that the woman was now holding. It looked like a thick black snake, but it was too short, too rigid, like a baton you'd beat someone with. It was so thick that the woman couldn't fit her sausage-like fingers completely around the circumference of the object. Unlike a baton, though, Emma noticed it had a rounded cue-ball end and veins ran along its length, which Emma estimated to be at least twelve inches.

Emma's breath choked when she realized what the object was in the woman's hand. It was huge, grotesque. Haley Mitchell, one of Emma's friends, had laughed about owning one when she had shown Emma. "Who needs a man when you can have one of these?" Haley had chuckled a few weeks back when she had pulled the thick, rubberized male appendage from her bedside drawer.

But the one the woman was holding was twice as long, and a lot thicker. Clearly, this version was designed for inflicting pain, not pleasure.

Emma felt nauseous just looking at the ugly thing.

The woman brought it up and waved it at Emma, an evil smile spreading across her face, the meaty jowls of her jaw quivering in greedy delight. "You didn't comply, did you, Emma?" she questioned, like a schoolteacher reprimanding a naughty student.

Emma swallowed hard. Her eyes darted to the toolbox where the hammer sat. Could she reach it in time? Then she realized she didn't need to. She smiled at the woman. "Come on, then. Let's see how far you can slide that inside me." Emma parted her legs slightly and raised an eyebrow. "I'm getting all wet just thinking about it."

A look of surprise shot across the woman's face. She licked her lips, then advanced on Emma. "Good," she said. "It's wise to accept your punishment."

Emma glanced past the woman. The heavy steel door was wide open. Now was her chance. She looked back at the woman, then in a husky voice, said, "I'll do whatever you want. I need to be punished." Emma pivoted her left hip forward slightly and dropped into a subtle fighting stance. "Come here, Dolly, and punish me." Emma gave an inviting tilt of her head. "Do it right, or I'll make you do it again and again until you do."

Pure delight filled Dolly's eyes as she shuffled forward eagerly.

And when she was within reach, Emma unleashed.

16

MEMENTO MORI

"She also has a tattoo," Karen Block says to me.

"A tattoo?"

"Yeah."

Karen indicates to the inside of her right forearm. "It's a skull and something else. I never paid much attention to it. Damn ugly, if you ask me." She scowls, her mouth downturned. "Emma had it done a few years back. I wasn't happy because she was below the legal age." She gives an exasperated sigh. "But what can you do? If you remove it, it will leave a damn scar. And Emma is not the type of person to be told what to do either."

I'm not sure what the significance is of the tattoo. It's not like I've asked Karen if there are any distinguishing marks on her daughter because I've got a body in the morgue to be identified—yet. "Do you have any photos of the tattoo?" I ask. "Maybe of Emma where I can see it clearly?"

Karen lifts a heavy-looking photo album from a drawer, then begins flipping through it. A few moments later she pauses, then hands me the open album. "There. Taken last summer." She points to a particular photo. Tanned and wearing a skimpy bikini, and dripping with water, Emma is standing on a boulder near a waterfall. Her face is all sunshine and rainbows, white teeth, and sun-bronzed vitality. Her torso is twisted away from the camera, and I can clearly see the inside of her right forearm where three symbols are aligned from the elbow crease toward her wrist. I tilt the album clockwise ninety degrees because the symbols are oriented horizontally in line with the arm. I squint at the picture, then look up at Karen. "Is it okay if I take a photo?"

She nods, then looks away.

Taking out my cell phone, I take several photos as best I can from different distances and various camera modes, making sure each picture is as clear as I can possibly make it, given that I'm taking a picture of a picture. After I'm done, I scroll through the pictures I've taken, scrutinizing each one.

There are three dark green tattoos, no color infill. A skull is in the middle and is flanked by an hourglass on one side and a wilting flower in a vase on the other.

Odd.

I've seen a lot of tattoos in my day, especially gang-related, but nothing like this. Perhaps it's Greek, symbolic of something? There's no wording to give a clue as to the meaning. I quickly shoot off the best photo to Vega. Maybe she can decipher what the tattoo means.

Thanking Karen Block, I return to my rental that's parked at the curb, and even before I can unlock the door, my cell pings. It's Vega, with a cryptic quote.

Memento mori. Remember, you must die.

"Remember you must die," I whisper the words to myself. Now the tattoo makes sense. The skull obviously represents death, our mortality. Inside my car, I think about the meaning some more. The hourglass represents the passing of time, a precious resource. Don't waste it. Every moment a few more grains are trickling by. It can have a multitude of meanings all leading to the same interpretation. Do not waste your life. Life is precious. Live life to the fullest.

The wilting flower has a similar but slightly different connotation,

I imagine. It represents life as well, but life that is slowly dying. From the day you are born, you start dying. With each grain of sand that passes through the hourglass, you are getting closer to your own death. A lot of people don't realize that. Every minute of every hour of every day, you are slowly dying. Some people accelerate the process. It's morbid, I know. But it has such a raw clarity to it that Emma wanted it tattooed on the inside of her forearm so she could be reminded of it each day.

Instinctively, I touch the side of my head and am reminded of my own mortality. I can almost feel it there, lurking beneath my skull bone, the poison, the tumor, growing slowly, getting larger and more invasive each day.

Memento mori. Remember, you must die.

And yet I haven't noticed my own strength wilting. The opposite, in fact. I feel good, strong, and more determined now.

According to my oncologist, I can't escape this death that's now plaguing me. But maybe I can help Emma Block escape her certain death, a death that has been brought on far too early for one so young. She'll die one day. We all do. I want Emma to grow old, much older than me. To have kids, too, to start a family, like how I've always wanted to but haven't told anyone. Being so absorbed in my career and my own pigheadedness has been a natural birth control pill I've swallowed for so long that men have run a mile from me.

All but one.

I think about Ben Shaw for a moment. Should I tell him? What good would it do? Maybe we could have one last fling before I leave this earth. The thought of that possibility brings a smile to my face, but it quickly dissolves into a frown.

Dread suddenly fills me. Could Emma be already dead? I don't think so. Call it intuition, yet for some reason, deep down inside me, I believe she's still alive. And just like the sands spilling through the hourglass, she hasn't got much time left on this earth. All of Pritchard's victims have died within two or three days of being taken, and we're almost past that now. He makes no exceptions. None have ever escaped to tell the tale. Once he has you in his grasp, it's a short stint on death row while he has his fun with you before he pulls your plug for good.

Emma Block and I are now connected. We share a common bond; death is breathing down both our necks. And if she's still managed to stay alive, has become the one exception, she as sure as hell is not going to die before me. I make that vow right now.

She will *not* die before me.

Through the windshield, I stare off into the distance. She's out there, somewhere, alive, her heart still beating. For how much longer, I'm not sure.

I need to find her.

Memento mori.

I start the car, my jaw tight with anger, my fingers bone-white on the steering wheel, imagining they're wrapped around Sam Pritchard's throat.

She will *not* die before me.

Emma's life is not his for the taking. I've escaped death. Now I'm going to make sure she does, too, if it's the last thing I do.

And it probably will be.

17

FANGED VAMPIRES

Emma had practiced the particular kick thousands of times, a majority of which were on a heavy punching bag. She was right-handed, but for some strange reason, her left roundhouse kick was cleaner, harder, and more accurate than her right.

During an All-Styles tournament in Tallahassee, she had pulled it out in the third round to win the bout and ultimately the first-place trophy. Her opponent was a man, a lot older, and much bigger, who, despite the light-contact rules, was steamrolling her with aggressive kicks and punches almost at full-contact pace. The final straw had been a deliberately aimed punch to one of her breasts that sent her gasping in pain to her knees on the mat. After getting back on her feet, Emma knew what she had to do. So, when the referee shouted for them to engage again, Emma buried the instep of her left foot deep into the man's face in a perfectly timed and surgically executed round-house kick, much to the cheer of the audience, knocking him out cold.

Thankfully, it was Emma's right ankle and not her left that was still chained. The slack in the chain wasn't much, but it was enough. She waited until the very last moment, when Dolly was easily within reach, then unfurled a beautifully timed and lightning-fast roundhouse kick to the woman's fat head with her left foot while her chained right foot was firmly planted on the ground.

And just like with her opponent in Tallahassee, she swiveled her hips well past the point of impact, like her sensei had told her to, imagining that she was booting a watermelon off a tree stump and into the next county. In this instance, the watermelon was Dolly's skull perched on her thick neck, which was protruding out of her squat body. The wet, smacking noise of her foot striking Dolly's head was music to Emma's ears.

Dolly's head jerked violently sideways as bone and cartilage shattered under the full force of the kick. Like a puppet with its strings suddenly snipped, Dolly collapsed into an ungainly heap on the floor.

Dolly had fallen backward and away from her, so Emma dragged the bed until she stood over her. "Lights out, bitch." Quickly, Emma began searching through the woman's clothing.

The keys! The keys must be here!

Her fingertips touched something cold and metallic inside one pocket.

Keys! Hope bloomed inside Emma.

Three differently shaped keys hung from a thick brass ring she pulled from the pocket. She found the correct key to finally free herself from the shackle around her ankle and tossed the chain aside, then looked down at the unconscious form of Dolly at her feet. Blood was dripping from Dolly's nose and mouth, and she looked dead. Picking up the chain and winding it around both of her hands, Emma hovered over Dolly. It would be so easy to just loop the chain around the woman's throat and crush her neck like a chicken's just to make sure. God knows she deserved to die.

Emma lowered the chain, then unfurled it from her hands, letting it drop to the floor. She just wanted to get out of there as fast as she could. Then there was the old man who had abducted her to think about. He must be lurking nearby.

The heavy steel door to her cell had been left open, but Emma kept the bunch of keys just in case. She didn't know what other locked doors she would encounter during her escape. On the other side of the steel door, a set of concrete stairs led upward. At the top, she found another heavy steel door left ajar. Dolly must have been so confident that she hadn't bothered closing any of the doors behind her, Emma thought as she ran through the next doorway before finding herself in a tunnel-like passageway. It was dimly lit by old filament bulbs in caged enclosures that ran the length of the curved stone ceiling above her head.

Don't stop! Keep going! Emma sped along the passageway, then up another set of metal stairs this time, her feet clanging as she climbed. The stairs ended at another door made of old steel tarnished with age, which looked like some kind of airlock. The door had a thick spinning wheel at its center, the kind you would expect to see sunken into a submarine hatch. Emma turned the wheel until she could feel the door separate from the rubber housing of the jamb, then pushed the door open.

A crack of sunlight streamed in, and Emma pushed the door outward, farther on its heavy hinges—then paused.

Turning back, she looked down the metal stairs she had just climbed. Was that a sound she had just heard? Like a door being slammed shut? Gooseflesh ripped across her skin.

Wasting no more time, she stepped through the opening.

Closing her eyes, Emma inhaled deeply. *Fresh air! The sun! Clear skies!* The relief of being finally free from her underground prison overwhelmed her, and tears welled behind her eyelids.

She had escaped.

But where was she?

Opening her eyes, she wiped away her tears. She was in a large clearing surrounded by heavily wooded forest. On the opposite side of the clearing, a small log cabin sat nestled: its tin roof dappled in golden sunlight with a ghostly tendril of smoke twisting up from a chimney. It all seemed like a dream; the log cabin was so picturesque, the warm sunlight, the birds singing, yellow butterflies dancing above a carpet of wildflowers growing beneath the trees.

Then her eyes picked out the dark pickup truck almost hidden among the shadows near the log cabin. It was the same pickup truck the old man was driving when he had pulled over to where Emma had broken down on the side of the road.

Dread hit Emma, and instantly, the warm, surreal spring vista turned into a frigid, cold arctic wasteland. The sun became a blood moon. The birdsong now sounded more like the raspy cry of ravens. The wildflowers withered into black, papery dead stalks, and the yellow butterflies morphed into furious, fanged vampire bats that began swooping toward her.

He was inside the log cabin. Emma knew it. She could almost feel his thick, evil presence seeping out of the gaps between the hewn cabin logs, spewing out of the chimney above, and oozing between the sides of the window frames.

Then the front door of the log cabin slowly opened.

18

EAT THIS

Run! Run! Emma's brain began screaming.

But to where?

The cabin door paused, not fully open, not fully closed, ajar just a few inches as though someone were looking out, hesitating before stepping outside as if they had heard a noise and were checking to make sure.

Move, you dumb, doe-eyed shit! The impatient half of Emma's brain screamed it again. Like a jackrabbit, Emma bounded off toward the tree line on her right, sprinting as fast as she could, cutting off the line of sight he may have had of her as he looked out his cabin door.

Shadows fell on Emma as she plunged into the tree line. Low branches clawed across her face and arms as she ran and took up position behind the first large tree she could find. Then, after molding her spine against the trunk, she tried to calm her breathing, praying that whoever had opened the cabin door hadn't seen her. She counted to ten before carefully pivoting her head around the curve of the trunk and glancing back toward the cabin.

The clearing was empty, so was the cabin porch. She couldn't see the cabin door from the angle where she was hiding. That was a good thing because it also meant he couldn't see her. Maybe he had. Maybe he was faking it, pretending he hadn't glimpsed her standing like a dumbass deer in the headlights, slap-bang in the middle of the clearing before dashing off into the undergrowth. Right now he could be back inside the cabin grabbing a big knife or baseball bat and at any moment was going to emerge and come after her.

The birds had stopped tweeting. The light breeze had died. Even the insects had taken a break from their incessant grating. There were no other sounds at all. No dull background hum of traffic. No distant shrill of a siren or moan of a truck horn. Not even the faint echoing rumble of a jetliner high in the sky. It was all just wilderness, which was now unnervingly silent.

A single icy rivulet of sweat trickled down Emma's temple as she watched the cabin for any signs of the man.

The pickup was parked at the end of the dirt road. Surely that would lead to a major road or highway, and once there, she could flag down a passing motorist. Following the dirt road would expose her, however. A few butterflies fluttered between the surrounding trees, making her present situation seem absurdly calm and tranquil, despite her heart doing chest compressions against the inside of her rib cage.

Farther back in the clearing, Emma caught sight of a squat concrete, wedge-shaped structure that looked like someone had pushed it up through the earth. It had a dark opening and a hinged door with a turning wheel. Now she realized where she had emerged from. The structure protruding from the ground looked like the entrance to a fallout shelter. They had imprisoned her underground.

Her eyes returned to the pickup. Should she take it? It would certainly be an easier ride out of here than on foot. She could drive fast to the nearest town or a gas station and call the police. If she ran deeper into the woods, she'd get lost, disorientated, and he would find her. She had seen enough horror movies to know that no matter how fast you ran in the woods, or how dark it was, the killer somehow always found you. She didn't know who the old guy was, but she had a nasty feeling he would hunt her down and catch her again.

She checked the keys she had taken off Dolly. None of them looked like a car key. *There goes that idea.*

There was still no activity on the cabin porch. Had he gone back inside?

The dark opening of the fallout shelter yawned like a sinister, cruel mouth. The man was going to get suspicious if the old woman didn't emerge from there soon.

Emma was about to edge forward when the front door of the cabin opened and the old man appeared, walking to the top of the stairs before pausing.

Emma tensed, then ducked back behind the tree trunk. *The bastard!* He and the old witch were definitely a tag team. *Bonnie and fucking Clyde.*

Peering again around the tree trunk, Emma felt her chest tightening as she watched him standing on the porch, gazing across the clearing toward the fallout shelter. He was thinking while rubbing his chin. Looking annoyed, he descended the stairs and began walking toward the shelter, cussing under his breath.

Emma rotated around the trunk as the man moved, ensuring she remained hidden while watching his movements with one eye peeking out from the curved edge. He then stepped through the open hatch and vanished into the fallout shelter.

Now! She only had a few minutes at the most before he would discover the old woman on the floor.

Breaking cover, Emma sprinted across the clearing toward the cabin, then up the porch stairs and through the door, closing it gently behind her. Her eyes darted around. Two wooden chairs. Threadbare rug. A wooden table with an open box of caramel Ding Dongs. Compact kitchen. A woodstove with a coffee pot bubbling on the warmer.

Ding-fucking-Dongs! Emma knew it was dumb, stupid, an incredibly dangerous waste of precious seconds. But she hadn't eaten in days, and her stomach balled into a fist at the sight of the open box of small, fudge-covered cakes with the caramel-creme filling. She ripped open one packet and stuffed the entire cake in her mouth, then pocketed another two before searching around the inside of the cabin.

There was no key hook near the front door. *No, that would have been too easy.* No car keys on the kitchen counter. Nothing on the small wooden table either. Maybe he'd taken the keys with him, she thought while stuffing another Ding Dong into her mouth.

The room spun as panic rose inside Emma.

Shit! Shit! Shit!

She stole a quick look out of the window next to the door. The dark opening of the fallout shelter glared back at her like a huge, one-eyed skull. No sign of him. How long had it been? Thirty seconds? A minute? Fear makes an easy liar of time.

Frantically, she started pulling out kitchen drawers and rummaging through cutlery. A knife sliced her hand. *Fuck!*

No keys.

The overhead cupboards were next. A pottery coffee mug slipped past her probing fingers and fell to the floor, shattering with a jarring crack. Startled, Emma whirled around, her heart beating faster, and spotted a jacket draped off the back of one of the wooden chairs.

The keys must be in there. Quickly, she rifled through the pockets, panic boiling faster up her throat now. Inside one pocket, her fingers found a plastic fob, and she pulled out a car key, then threw the jacket aside.

Yes! She almost wept with relief. Now she could get the hell out of here.

The cabin door kicked open behind her, then slammed hard against the wall.

Standing in the doorway was the old man, his arm wrapped around the woman. Her jaw sagged on one side, unhinged, giving her face a skull-like appearance. Long strands of bloody drool stretched down her crooked chin, and the right side of her face bulged like a football had inflated itself under the skin.

The man's dark eyes glowered at Emma, and she felt as though the devil had just wrapped his pointy, black tongue around her soul.

Shrugging off the man's arm, Dolly shambled toward Emma like a zombie, globules of thick red saliva dripping from her chin and onto the floor.

"I'm g...gonna," Dolly stuttered, her crooked jaw quivering. "C...cut out your c...cunt and feed it to ya."

19

HEAD IN THE MICROWAVE

The late afternoon sun is throwing dark shadows across me as I stand under the steel awning covering the gas station pumps, my eyes searching for any clues that could lead me to where Sam Pritchard is right now. There are only a few cars pulled into the forecourt: a white pickup truck, a red sun-faded sedan, and a minivan, the drivers all of which are either pumping gas or returning from buying food and drinks at the store.

He was here, right where I'm standing, not more than two days ago, and it's like I can feel him, his residue, sticky and lurid, hanging in the air around me. A twenty-four-hour diner sits next to the gas station, and I try to visualize him walking across in front of me, maybe giving me a friendly nod before climbing into his RAM pickup.

I perform a slow rotation, taking in everything again, the sounds, the smells, paying particular attention to the entrance and exit points. Where did he come from? And where did he go? He couldn't have gone too far, given that he's now driving a pickup truck and not some big eighteen-wheeler that he used to drive with a modified hidden slide-out tray under the chassis, where he transported his drugged victims. It would be so difficult for him to hide Emma in his pickup truck now without being caught. So, my gut is telling me he hasn't gone far.

The landscape surrounding the gas station is flat farmland. Maybe he has found another mine tunnel like he did in Utah?

There are three external security cameras as far as I can tell: two under the awning that covers the pumps, and a third over the entrance to the store. From the video footage Vega lifted, Pritchard was alone. There was no one in the passenger seat of his pickup, so he wouldn't have grabbed Emma first before coming here and filling up with gas. No. He came here first, then went out hunting, happened upon her by chance. Emma didn't come here, so her breaking down on the side of the road was pure bad luck and his demented good fortune.

But where did he hide her in the pickup? The model of RAM he drives has a six-foot open box with a tailgate. He wouldn't have simply thrown her in the bed and covered her with a blanket, hoping no one would notice.

Chloroform is his drug of choice for subduing his victims. It can render you unconscious from twenty minutes and up to two hours, if reapplied. Too concentrated a dose, and it can easily kill you. As past autopsies will attest, Pritchard hasn't made that mistake. He is too clever, too meticulous, too careful. Which also means he wouldn't have driven too far from where the Honda was discovered a few miles up the road from here.

Performing another walk around the forecourt, I can't help thinking that I'm missing something, a vital clue that I just need to find.

My cell phone rings, and I check the screen. My heart sinks a little but not too deep, just below the surface of my frustration, where it's content to tread water for a while. Unlike before, I decide to take the call this time because I've already rejected three previous attempts today from the same caller.

The voice on the end of the line sounds annoyingly cheerful

despite the context. "Miss. Ryder? It's Gail Summers from Dr. Green's office."

Of course it is. Gail doesn't give me a chance to answer. She just barrels right on with the reason for the call, which I suspected anyway.

"Dr. Green has asked me to follow up with you. It looks like you haven't made an appointment for your first treatment session. It's been almost a week now."

I'm not sure if the last sentence is a question or a reprimand. It's not her fault. She's just doing her job. What excuse can I give her? That I've got some more pressing matters to attend to instead of having my brain nuked with radiation? Such as hunting down the Highway Killer, because he took an eighteen-year-old woman a few days ago, and time is of the essence.

I almost burst out laughing when Gail adds, "And time is of the essence."

No shit, Einstein—I mean, Marie Curie.

It sounds incredibly stupid, but I say it anyway. "Look, I'm sorry. I've been very busy. It's not a good time for me at the moment." *Yeah, dying can take a rain check for now.*

As I expect, there's a pause on the other end, and I imagine Gail is cycling through her brain, trying to rationalize what could be more important than slowing down an aggressive brain tumor so I can live a little longer. My own rationale is equivalent to standing in front of a freight train. Why try to slow something down that can't be stopped? It's going to kill me—the brain tumor, that is—eventually. Maybe after I catch Pritchard, I will stand in front of a freight train. The thought of seeing my hair fall out and my body cannibalizing itself as I watch myself slowly wither and die isn't that appealing.

I follow up with an equally stupid but true statement. "At the moment, I'm actually feeling good."

Again, the lengthy pause and then a more clipped, direct response. "I understand that, Miss. Ryder. However, Dr. Green believes that the treatment is worthwhile. It may delay—"

Gail doesn't end the sentence, and I almost suggest that she should get a tattoo. I have a particular one in mind. Maybe Dr. Green could also get the same one.

Memento mori. Remember, you must die. But I imagine it would be bad for business.

Now I'm just being a cynical bitch. I am better than that. "Look," I say, "I understand your concern." The referral I trashed has probably made it to the landfill by now. I don't tell Gail that, however.

I end the call by telling Gail that I will try to make an appointment by the end of the week. I make no promises, no commitments, because the only commitment I've made so far is to myself and to Emma Block. And that commitment is the only one I can manage for the moment.

Nothing else, including sticking my head inside a microwave, matters to me.

20

NO WAY OUT

Emma backed away some more until she felt the edge of the kitchen counter cut into her back.

"Stay away from me, you bitch, otherwise I'll take your head off this time," she growled at Dolly.

The words seemed to have little effect on the woman with the crooked jaw. "W...will you j...just?" The bottom half of her face wobbled like some grotesque Halloween mask. Rummaging among the folds of her clothing, Dolly produced a switchblade and sprang the knife open with a sickening click. "I should've c...cut your t...tits off when I had the chance," she stuttered, admiring the blade. Her eyes focused back on Emma. "Now I'm going to cut *everything* off." She pointed the tip of the blade at Emma's groin. "Starting with that!" She spoke over her shoulder to the man. "Grab her and hold her down for me."

He didn't move. "Dolly, I told you we should've killed her sooner."

"Shut up!" she said. "I want to keep her for a while." Dolly's eyes narrowed. Her tongue slithered out, and her jaw gave a clicking sound as she licked her lips at Emma. "What a succulent young thing you are," she crooned. Then her face hardened. "Now, do as I say, Pritchard, and hold her down."

Pritchard? Emma thought. At least she knew his name now. Dolly was obviously in charge. She wanted to keep Emma as her plaything, whereas he wanted to kill her much sooner. Both fates seemed equally bad to Emma.

Dolly turned and glared at Pritchard. "I told you to fucking grab the bitch!" She tilted her head up at Pritchard. "What's up? Suddenly got an attack of the guilts?" she said mockingly, her words wet and thick, her voice wavering between normal but hindered pronunciation and garbled syllables with no edge to the words.

"You told me you enjoyed torturing women. That it's b...better than s...sex." Her jaw clicked as she spoke.

Pritchard shook his head. "Not like this. This is not what I wanted, and you know it. I took her for you. I wanted to kill her sooner. This wasn't in my plan, to keep her this long."

Dolly raised her eyebrows. "Your plan? You don't have a f... fucking plan. It was me who f...found you, gave you direction, put some order into your pathetic little life. You were just driving around picking up women with no rhyme or reason."

Emma glanced around, looking for a way to get out of the cabin while the two argued. Front door? That was now out of the question. Both of them stood between her and the door. Both of them were a good sixty to seventy pounds heavier than her. Even if she got past Dolly, she'd still have him to contend with. Despite his age, he was built like a grizzly bear, broad-shouldered, with thick forearms and hands like a pitcher's mitt.

Window, maybe? There were two of them on either side of the room, and one next to the front door. But they were all closed, latched shut. It would take her precious seconds to unlock and slide them up and climb out. However, the thin wood-cross frames looked flimsy. Maybe she could take a running dive through the glass, like in the movies, and tumble outside. What about a back door? She didn't see one. Then again, she never looked when she first entered. She just wanted to find the keys. *The keys!* Emma still had them in her hand and instinctively closed her fingers over them, hiding them from sight. They felt hot and clammy in her fist. They weren't a weapon, though, and would be no match for the switchblade Dolly was wielding.

"You're taking too long," he said to Dolly.

"Really?" Dolly scoffed, bloody drool spilling from her chin. "How long did you keep that girl in that cave in Utah, you bragged about?"

A girl in a fucking cave? A door in Emma's mind opened, revealing a whole new closetful of horrors.

Pritchard went silent.

"You had your fun with her, didn't you? You didn't kill her right away."

Emma stole a quick look behind her into the small kitchen. A bread knife sat on a wooden cutting board, next to a half-sliced loaf and an open jar of Jif peanut butter. She glanced back at the other two. Dolly had now turned and was facing Pritchard. Both of them seemed to have forgotten about Emma and were taking swipes at each other. That suited her just fine. An inch at a time, she edged sideways along the counter toward the end, where she could get to the bread knife.

Pritchard affixed Dolly with an icy stare. "That was different, and you know it."

Dolly gave a choking laugh. "Different? How is that any different?" She was now pointing the switchblade knife at Pritchard.

With her eyes fixed on the two, Emma moved another few inches. She had reached the edge of the counter. In her mind, she pictured the bread knife on the cutting board, envisaged herself spinning around, and making a leap for it. It couldn't be more than three feet away. Two quick strides and she would have it.

Dolly continued scolding Pritchard. "And that mother of three you kept in that furnace of a grain silo, for what, three days?"

"She was special," Pritchard replied, his fists now bunched.

As if to prove a point, Dolly wheeled around to face Emma, bringing the knife back up and pointing it at her. "She's special, too," Dolly said.

Emma froze. Her heart was beating so hard she thought she was going into cardiac arrest. If she didn't escape now, she never would. Her abduction wasn't just some random muse. These two maniacs were seasoned killers who enjoyed kidnapping, torturing, then murdering people.

Dolly frowned at Emma as though just noticing her for the first time.

Emma held her breath, unsure whether Dolly had noticed she had shifted her position along the kitchen bench.

Dolly tilted her head at Emma but said nothing, a look of curiosity in her dark eyes.

Pritchard reached behind his back and pulled something from the waistband of his trousers.

Stepping up next to Dolly, he smacked a coil of rough rope in his palm. "Let's get this over and done with, Dolly," he said, relenting to her wishes.

"Good," Dolly replied, looking at the rope in Pritchard's hands. "Now hog-tie the bitch."

Dolly turned her attention back to Emma, raising the knife up even higher. "And don't worry," she continued, addressing Pritchard but keeping her eyes firmly on Emma. "She'll be dead by the time the sun sets today, and we'll be out of here." Dolly took a step toward Emma. "And by my calculation, that will be within the next two hours. But until then, I do not want to waste a single second of it." Another strand of bloody drool stretched from her mouth. "And by the time I'm f...finished, Miss Pretty Tits here is gonna look like human roadkill."

Emma sprang sideways, pivoted, then leaped into the kitchen toward the bread knife. Snatching it up, she twisted around, holding the knife out in front of her. "Touch me and I'll kill you both!" she hissed like a cornered alley cat.

Dolly seemed amused by the threat, while Pritchard began advancing toward Emma, the rope in one hand.

"Stay away! Stay away!" Emma yelled, waving the knife. "I'm warning you."

Seemingly undeterred, Pritchard stepped into the kitchen, a killer's soulless look in his eyes.

Emma looked wildly around, then spotted a small door covered by a frilly, red curtain at the back of the kitchen. She took a step backward, waving the knife at Pritchard as he advanced. "I will kill you," she screamed.

"I doubt that," Pritchard replied, with all the cool calmness of a man who had subdued many women before Emma.

Releasing a manic scream, Emma sprang forward, deciding that attack was the best form of defense, and lunged at Pritchard, aiming the knife at the center of his throat.

21

A PLACE OF SCREAMING

After grabbing a paper map of the local area from the gas station, I head inside the diner and take a seat in a booth near the window.

Almost immediately, a waitress appears, places a coffee mug down, and fills it with steaming black coffee. I haven't eaten since yesterday, and my stomach cramps suddenly with hunger from the smell of the coffee. Like the rest of the diner, the name tag she is wearing—*Frances*—has lost its shine and is faded with age. By contrast, her uniform is bright, neat, and freshly starched. I can't say the same for the rest of the staff: a disheveled bunch who seem to be holding a town meeting next to the cash register, the air around them thick with whining about poor tips and rising inflation, all of whom ignored me when I entered.

"What can I get you, honey?" Frances asks. She is maybe in her late sixties, three times the average age of her fellow staff, by my estimate, and reeks of a hardworking, no-nonsense work ethic that is sadly missing in society today. Petite, with wispy corn-colored hair, attentive eyes, she possesses a genuine smile I know won't flip to a downward frown the moment she turns away from me. She seems like a local, has that kind of face that's seen a lifetime of diners, yet her mood is upbeat, has a glass-half-full tempo to it. Reading glasses hang from a pink plastic chain around her neck that is decorated with tiny blue-sequined butterflies.

Quickly, I flip through the huge trifold laminate menu and order a breakfast burrito. The denser the calories, the better, if I'm going to keep going with very little sleep. And I've noticed that I've lost a few pounds in the last few days. Getting sick is the best form of dieting.

Frances smiles and juts her pen at the unfolded map on the table. "Where are you heading to, honey?"

Obviously, everyone must just pass through here on the way to somewhere else. On the drive here, there wasn't much else worth noting. "I'm not sure yet."

"I'll put your order in right away," she says before turning and heading to the open kitchen window. The town meeting by the cash register is more animated now, with vigorous hand gestures and a few eye rolls thrown in for good measure.

There's another security camera perched behind the cash register and one in the far back corner above a restroom sign. Vega has already checked the footage. Pritchard didn't come into the diner. He grabbed his coffee from the gas station instead, so I guess there's no point in asking any of the staff about him. People these days tend to keep to themselves as well. He would have looked like any of the other lonely highway travelers I've already seen, filling up his pickup after paying for the gas and moving on. He would've known about the security cameras, too, under the ceiling of the forecourt overhang and those inside the store. But didn't seem to care. Being confident, but not overly, is another one of his traits.

While drinking my coffee, I look out the window for the next few minutes, but there's nothing else I can glean, from what I see. It's not as if Pritchard dropped some huge clue here just for me to discover. That's the problem with him. The clues are very few, and he tends not to drop them at all. You almost have to wrestle them from his murderous grasp, then catch them before they fall into the cracks in the earth under which he buries his victims.

Unfolding the map, I smooth it out. At times I prefer using an actual paper map, spreading it out, so I can take in the full expanse of a search area in one go rather than having to be constantly sliding around with one finger over a small section of a much larger digital map on my cell phone.

The city of Camilla, where Karen and her daughter live, lies thirteen miles to the east, and there's not much else within a twenty-mile radius: a scattering of small churches, an irrigation plant, two produce stores, and a cemetery. Pritchard is nomadic now, so he doesn't have the fixed seclusion of the farmhouse and barn of horrors he once had with his last permanent address. That makes him even more difficult to find. Now I imagine he makes do with what he can find on the open road. Hidden, long-forgotten places where he can quickly transport his victims while they are still unconscious. Secluded spots where no one can disturb him. That would exclude private property, storage areas, or commercial places with security cameras, where he knows he doesn't belong. Public places such as gas stations, roadside diners, motels, and shopping malls where he can move freely, blend in with the rest of the masses.

I scour the map, knowing full well it will not reveal the details of such places that would be perfect for him to safely keep Emma: disused buildings, abandoned mines, empty structures long since abandoned. Such locations and others like them must also offer a certain degree of invisibility from a main road and someplace where he can safely hide his pickup, too.

The surrounding area is mainly irrigated farmland, and there is a large wooded area, a state forest, a few miles north of here with the Flint River running through it. But the map isn't detailed enough to show smaller structures such as disused cabins, barns, and the like.

Frances returns with my food, and I push the map to one side.

"You look like you're looking for someplace," she says, placing down the large plate—and a bowl of fries that I didn't order. She gives me a good-natured nudge with her elbow and winks at me. "Honey, you're all skin and bone," she whispers. "The fries are on the house."

"Thanks." Am I really wasting away? I make a note to check myself out in the mirror the next time I go to the restroom.

"If you're into sightseeing," she continues, shaking her head, "there's nothing much to see around here."

I pause and look up at her. "Are you from around here?"

"Born and bred, honey."

I think for a moment. What have I got to lose? Apart from Vega placing Pritchard in this location around the same time Emma Block broke down, we have no other clues. The police haven't bothered to visit Emma Block's mother, and why would they? They think Emma is just a wayward teenager who will return home soon. And Karen Block doesn't seem to be too bothered by her daughter's disappearance, only lodging a missing-persons report just to teach her daughter a lesson for taking her car without asking.

"I'm looking for someone who has gone missing," I finally say, then wait for a look of surprise on Frances's face. Nothing materializes. Maybe a lot of people go missing around here, so people don't bat an eyelid when asked. "I could really do with some help."

Frances gives me a motherly smile. "You're not from around here, honey, are you?"

"Nope. But I'd appreciate it if you could help me."

"Sure, honey." She leans in and studies the map. "You say this person has gone missing, like run off or something or got lost?"

"Not exactly."

Frances gives me a sideways look, her brow furrowed.

I take a deep breath. Like I said, I've got nothing to lose, and the clock is ticking. I tap the map with my finger.

"Frances, I need to know where *you* would take someone, say, within a five-to-ten-mile radius of here if you had just kidnapped them, and you didn't want them or yourself to be found."

Frances raises an eyebrow, and a sparkle germinates in her eyes.

What I say next is not meant to be dramatic or to shock her. I simply say it because it's true. "A quiet, secluded location where you can take that person and where no one can hear their screams."

22

CRUEL TOYS

Emma didn't get more than a foot toward Pritchard when a ring of hot molten steel encircled the wrist of her hand that was holding the bread knife.

She tried pulling her hand free, but it didn't budge. Her arm just hung out in front of her as though the air surrounding it had suddenly turned into invisible cement, encasing it in stone.

Rapidly deploying several handhold breaks she had learned made no difference. Then with a frightening casualness, Pritchard's powerful fingers slid down and wrapped around her hand, forcing fragile bones in a direction they were not anatomically designed to be forced.

Emma screamed in pain and released the bread knife. It clattered to the floor.

Crooked-jawed and drooling blood, Dolly shambled forward again, brandishing the switchblade, a half-crazed look in her saucer-sized eyes. "Good. Now you hog-tie her like I said. But don't go busting up her pretty little face. A broken bone or two, I don't mind. But leave her face, and her sweet little pussy, to me."

Ignoring the searing pain that was coursing up her arm, and with Pritchard still holding her hand, Emma swung a left hook with her other hand, bunching her fingers into a tight knuckled fist, aiming it at his temple.

The first punch—nothing.

The second—the same.

On the third punch, Pritchard just grinned at her, the kind of grin that told her either his head was made of iron, or others had tried a similar tactic and had failed.

In one smooth motion, he spun her around like a ballroom dancer until her back was against him, then wrapped a bulging arm around her chest and drew her in, crushing her body against his.

Emma felt like someone had thrown a straitjacket over her head, cinching it tight. She tried to move, wriggle, twist, shake, anything. It was no good. It was barely enough to breathe.

Like a skilled rodeo rider, he wrapped the rope around one wrist, then forced the other wrist to join its mate, before wrapping them both in a bone-crushing figure eight.

Emma gasped as he lifted her off the ground and carried her out of the kitchen to where Dolly was waiting.

Dolly stepped forward and thrust the point of the switchblade at one of Emma's eyes, the tip of the blade just inches from the eyeball. "Maybe I should pluck this one out," she declared, her mouth making a wet, smacking sound. She nicked the air with the knife. "Or perhaps I should pluck them both out."

Emma twisted her head left, then right, trying to avoid the knife, but the point of the blade followed her movements. Gritting her teeth, she snarled, "Do whatever you want, slut!" Terror filled her, but she refused to show any sign of weakness. If she was going to die, then so be it. But she would not give the old witch the satisfaction of groveling for her life.

Dolly's gaze dropped to the inside of Emma's forearm. "What's this, then?" She glanced back up at Emma. "What does it mean, the symbols?"

Emma gritted her teeth. "It means *vete a la mierda. Fuck you* in Spanish."

Dolly's bottom jaw quivered as she leaned in, her face just inches from Emma's. "Tough little bitch, aren't you?"

The stench of raw sewage mixed with rancid meat flooded Emma's nose and mouth as Dolly's hot breath smothered her face. Specks of gooey spittle, tinged with blood, flew out of Dolly's crooked mouth and landed on Emma's cheeks and lips.

She lowered the knife, and Emma lost sight of it as it dropped below her chest. Moments later, she felt an inhuman violation as the tip of the blade was pressed into the cleft of her shorts.

"Let's see how tough you are when I start cutting this off," Dolly whispered. She nodded to Pritchard. "Take her back down and chain her to the bed again. I'll be there soon."

"You're injured," Pritchard replied. "You need to get that fixed." He pointed to her face.

"I ain't going to no ER!" Dolly gave a gurgling croak.

"I know how to put it back in place," he said. "There's a medicine chest under the sink. Some bandages and the like."

"Later!" Dolly said. "Just get her back and chain her up, then wait for me."

Turning, she regarded Emma once more. "I just need to get my toys."

23

DETONATION

"You a cop?"

I nod. Thankfully, Frances doesn't ask me for any ID. Why aren't people around here more suspicious of strangers? Maybe then someone would have paid more attention to Sam Pritchard. Then again, his outward behavior, I imagine, doesn't draw any untoward attention. He is a master of blending in, going unnoticed, with an uncanny knack of garnering your trust and putting you instantly at ease when he approaches you. That's why so many young women had probably felt so comfortable climbing up into his eighteen-wheeler when he had pulled over on the highway and offered them a ride. Little did they know they were climbing into their own funeral hearse with the devil himself behind the wheel.

"I'm Carolyn," I say, slipping a twenty out from my purse and placing it on the table.

It's not a snatch—as I've seen many people do when I flash some green to procure information—but a purposeful sleight of hand a magician would employ to make something vanish right before your very eyes—and it does, the twenty-dollar bill, right into some hidden pocket under her apron.

Good. Now we have an understanding.

"I could really use the help of someone who lives around here and has local knowledge. A young lady went missing not far from here a few days back. I believe she's been kidnapped and has only been taken a short distance." It's all speculation. For all I know, Emma Block could still be heavily sedated and halfway to Nebraska by now. But I doubt it.

"Well, I've certainly lived here all my life, Caroline," she says, then touches my arm. "I don't mean I've lived here in this diner all my life. But I grew up around these parts and haven't left."

I don't bother correcting her about my name. It doesn't matter. We won't be seeing each other again after this.

Frances leans over and points to where we are on the map. "This is us here." Then her face clouds over. "You say you're looking for a young woman who's been kidnapped, and you want to know a place close by where someone could've taken her."

It's like she's talking to herself, not asking me a question. "Like maybe an abandoned building or store," I suggest. "Someplace off the beaten track so to speak."

"A place where it's all private and the like." She gives her chin a thoughtful rub.

"Yes. Away from prying eyes."

Her own eyes narrow as she scrutinizes the map. "I must say, it's an unusual request you've made of me." Then both her eyebrows peak. "Maybe." She rubs her chin some more while staring at the map.

"Maybe, what?" I ask. It's like she is talking in riddles, seeing invisible locations on the map that only she has the power to see.

Frances lifts her glasses attached to the plastic chain around her neck and slides them on. Her voice sounds unsure when she speaks again. "It's been such a long time since I last looked at a map of the local area." Her face is now fixed with concentration, her finger hovering over the map. "And it's only a suggestion really," she says, "from what you've said, about kidnapping someone and where I would take them." Suddenly, she looks at me aghast. "Don't get me wrong. I would never in a million years kidnap someone."

The comment brings a smile to my lips. "Frances, I'm not saying that you would think about kidnapping someone. I just want to know where someone like yourself, who knows the local area, would hide someone."

"To do bad things to them?" Frances gives me a questioning look.

"Yes."

Her attention returns to the map, and then her finger taps a spot. "Here. Right here. It's obvious but it's not obvious, if you catch my drift."

Obvious but not obvious. I like that. Her finger comes to rest on an expanse of green. The wooded area I saw before with the Flint River running through it. The fizz of excitement fills me. Woods. Dark. Thick. Rambling. I thought about it before but didn't know if there was any place suitable within the woods, like an old logging plant or cave system or mine.

"There's an old log cabin up in these foothills," Frances continues. "Before it becomes state forest on the other side."

My excitement is immediately extinguished. *A cabin?* I wasn't thinking about a cabin. Maybe Frances has misunderstood what I'm looking for. Pritchard isn't exactly going to keep his prisoner in someplace as risky and as obvious as an old cabin in the woods, no matter how dark and isolated the cabin is. Pritchard wouldn't risk using an old cabin, even if it had been abandoned for a while. It's not his style.

"Don't get me wrong," Frances continues before I can voice my disappointment. "There's nothing special about this cabin."

My excitement hits rock bottom.

"But that's not what I meant," she says.

I look at her, and I see a faint glimmer of light amid the darkness.

She taps the map again. "The cabin itself isn't why I suggested the place."

The glimmer gets brighter as I listen intently to her. "What do you mean?"

"There's something else up there, near that particular cabin," she says triumphantly, drawing out the suspense. "Something that could be the perfect spot for hiding someone."

Our eyes meet. She leans in, then whispers. "An old cold-war fallout shelter. A big one, too. Lots of rooms and tunnels, so I've heard."

A nuclear bomb detonates inside my head, and I'm blinded by the sudden glare.

24

STONE-COLD DEAD

A fallout shelter?

My entire mouth is tingling, and a dark gray mist pours over me, making everything vanish. Frances. The map. The chipped laminate table it's sitting on. My coffee mug. The other chairs, tables, staff, windows, the entire diner, the sky and all the sunlight, evaporate into darkness. Then a tiny slither of light cuts through the black, getting larger and wider by the second, and I find myself drawn to it. The darkness splits apart, and I step through, finding myself in a drab room with walls skinned in filth and a floor thick with dust.

A fallout shelter. Yes!

Stale, earthy air coats the back of my throat, and it feels like I have a mouthful of soil and rotten mushrooms.

I see Emma. She's chained up.

Her clothes are torn, mere ribbons drenched in blood, barely covering the nakedness of her youth. Her hair, oily with sweat and nested with leaves and twigs, is covering her face. But through the matted strands, I can tell her eyes are closed. Her skin is deathly pale; her chest is still. Is she dead? Has this wretched place under the earth become her tomb?

Bending down, I brush aside her stiff bangs and touch her cheek. My fingertips feel icy cold, and a callous hand squeezes my heart.

She is dead. Stone...cold...dead.

I'm too late.

I have lost, and Pritchard has won. He always wins.

Then there's a ripple behind the underside of her eyelids, and they burst wide open.

I blink hard and am jolted back to the reality inside the diner with all its sights, sounds, and smells. But have I just witnessed reality?

Frances is looking down at me, concern in her eyes. "Where did you go, honey?" she asks.

I blink hard, then take a sip of water. Go? Where did I go? I...I... She's alive. I can feel it. My imagination just showed me. A fallout shelter. The last words Frances just said to me before I was transported someplace else. I can only imagine what that place must be like.

"Like a bunker, you mean?" I finally say. "Underground?"

Frances nods. "The old cabin up there used to belong to Gus Tanner. He died a few years back. From what I've heard, there are death taxes owed and the place is in limbo. No one can use it."

I glance down at the map. It certainly would be the perfect spot. Dark, dank, and creepy as hell. The perfect lair for Pritchard.

"Old Gus was always a bit of a conspiracy theorist," Frances goes on, topping up my coffee mug. "He built the fallout shelter back in the sixties, thinking that the Russians were going to invade." She waves the coffee pot around. "As if they're going to want to invade this place."

I look out the window. It will be dark soon. Maybe an hour of proper sunlight left. Two at the most. It may be spring, but the daylight hasn't yet stretched to its full zenith. Turning back to Frances, I ask, "What can you tell me about this fallout shelter?"

Frances gives a shrug. "Been up there a few times, but that was near on twenty years ago. Gus built it himself. Got a backhoe up there and everything, dug it out and poured the cement, he once told me. Proud as a bride, nine months after her wedding, he was. But after he died, the lawyers got involved. I guess no one went up there since." Her face morphs into a dreamy, faraway look. A slight smile touches the corners of her mouth as if she's reminiscing about fond memories. Long gone but not forgotten. "Gus always wanted to get into my panties," she says, her voice slow and measured. And with the flip of a switch, she's back in the present, all serious looking. Her eyes flare. "But I didn't let him, you know. He was always pestering me to go down into that hole in the ground, take a look with him. But I flatly refused. The thing scared the hell out of me."

"Thing?"

"It looks like one of those crypts rich people get buried in. The entrance is just a door, like a hatch sticking right up out of the ground. Creepy as all hell. God knows what he got up to down there after he finished building it. Always tinkering down there, I heard."

As far as I can tell from looking at the map, there's no road, trail, or otherwise leading to the place she is indicating. "So, how do I get up there?" I ask. "Can you give me directions?" Luckily, I've got some gear in the trunk of my rental car. Nothing major, though. Just a backpack with a change of clothes, flashlight, water, and some basic provisions. I don't know how long I'm going to be on the road for this trip. I don't have a weapon, no gun, nothing. It's difficult traveling with one, and I don't need the unwanted TSA attention.

Frances places her hand on her hip in contemplation. "Like I said, the last time I was up there was twenty years ago. It may be different now. As far as I can remember, there's a dirt road going up to it, just off the main road that curls around the base of the foothills. It may be overgrown now, but keep an eye out for it. There's no sign, nothing. The dirt road then forks. I think it's the left fork you take."

"Do you know where the other fork leads to?"

"Private property. Belongs to a local woman."

Before Frances lifts her finger off the map, I draw a circle around it, where the cabin should be, then scribble her directions on the map. While it all sounds promising, I don't want to get my hopes up, but the fallout shelter does sound more like Pritchard, dark places underground. Basements. Caves. Mines. My right thigh begins to ripple with gooseflesh at the thought of what happened under that mountain in Utah where Pritchard shot me in the leg, and I nearly bled out. I put five rounds into what I thought was him, standing there in the darkness only to have missed and for him to then vanish like a wraith —again. This time, however, I intend to finish him for good, send him to the fires of hell where he belongs.

I quickly push the past aside and return to the map. "And there are no other places, Frances? I just want to make sure."

She shakes her head. "If I was going to kidnap someone, that's where I would take them. I'm sure if you asked other locals around here, they'd say the same thing."

It makes me wonder, then, how Pritchard knew about the place. He's certainly not a local, yet he has proved himself time and time again to be very astute in finding grim, dark places that possess an unearthly solitude for him to do his sinister deeds. Maybe he's been through these parts before. I imagine he's always scouting for locations, noting them down in his sick, demented mind to be revisited later.

Folding up the map and gathering up my things, I thank Frances and head out to where my rental is parked, thinking about what the remainder of the day will bring before shooting off a quick text to Vega telling her what I've discovered.

25

MISSY

After opening the trunk of my rental, I check my backpack.

Then, unfolding the map, I hold it up and study again the location I had outlined with the circle I'd drawn around where Frances pointed her finger. Without warning, the details on the map blur, and the world tilts. I grab on to the lip of the trunk and try to steady myself as a sickening wave of giddiness wraps itself first around my eyes, then around my head. My mouth begins to salivate, a precursor to knowing what's coming next. Turning away, I manage to bend just in time before vomiting up my undigested breakfast burrito in a muddy swill of black coffee. Once, twice, three times, my stomach cramps and my throat retches, until there's nothing left inside me. Closing my eyes, I swallow hard and take a few deep breaths.

"You okay, ma'am?"

Without opening my eyes, I wave an *I'm fine* in the general direction of where the concerned voice came from.

"Geez, I was going to get something to eat at the diner"—the voice continues past me—"but I think I'll pass." The words of the good Samaritan fade away from where I'm bent over behind my car, my hands on my knees.

When I open my eyes again, the world has lost its tilt, and the sun is burning a brighter shade of orange. It's not food poisoning—and I'm not pregnant either. That would involve sex, and these days I can barely remember what that was once like. The nausea is subsiding, and the first fingers of fear, *real* fear, wrap around my heart, knocking my confidence, and infallibility, down a few pegs. Standing upright, I want to take my fist and punch the side of my head repeatedly to see if I can destroy, with my bare knuckles, the little evil cluster of abnormality that is lurking beneath my skin: cells that are dividing and multiplying without any control, and without my consent. It sounds stupid, I know, that perhaps I can bludgeon it into submission. But I'm angry and fearful. How dare this thing start growing inside me. I didn't give it permission.

Grabbing a water bottle from my backpack, I rinse my teeth and mouth, then count to ten while taking deep, calming breaths. If I'm going to remain in control, then I need to focus on the things I can control instead of the things I can't. I take another swallow of water. It tastes sour in my mouth, and the water inside the bottle is now speckled with floating bits of what I just ate.

Throwing the bottle into a nearby trash can, I then climb in behind the wheel and compose myself. Like the forewarning of an impending earthquake, the slight tremor I've just experienced has passed, and I start the engine, knowing full well that these bouts are going to increase in frequency and intensity—so I've been told—until eventually the earth splits open and the dark abyss claims me.

Pulling out of the gas station, I'm more determined on finding Pritchard and saving Emma.

MOVING out of the trees and to the edge, I look down onto the dry creek bed.

It must have once been a small tributary, running into the Flint

River, except there's no water here. It's now a motionless stream of sand, dirty silt, and stone that winds its way through the dense woodland. As far as I can tell, Gus Tanner's cabin must be on the opposite side, so I begin navigating my way down the slope, stumbling over loose rocks, my feet kicking free a small avalanche of scree that follows me down. It will be dark soon, and I don't fancy stumbling around in these woods then.

Reaching the bottom, I regain my balance and pull out the map again and check my location. Gus Tanner's log cabin must be there, maybe two hundred yards or so just past the lip of the bank on the other side. That is if Frances's directions are correct. I had parked my rental at the end of the dirt road I had found after following her directions. Then it was all on foot for about a mile through dense woodland, using the map and the compass on my cell phone.

Tucking the map away, I set off again, crawling and clawing my way up the opposite bank. It's much steeper, the earth more fragile. Using a few exposed roots that jut from the crumbling creek bank, I only just manage to hoist myself up and over before the roots snap off in my hand like brittle twigs.

A row of gnarly bushes at the top provides the perfect cover as I pause to get my bearings. Sweat bleeds down my back, and my mouth is dry. I remove my backpack and take a swig from a fresh water bottle. Will the fallout shelter be empty, or will Pritchard be there? And if he's there, will he have Emma with him? So far, it's been all speculation. And if he is there, I can't risk barging in. It's just me, alone, no backup that I've been used to having in the past. I don't want to forewarn him either. In my experience, the element of surprise can work both ways. After all this time, I'm not sure how I'm going to react when I do see him. He can just as well surprise me as I can surprise him. I know I've had training, that I'm supposed to remain calm, detached, act professional. All that can easily go flying out the window when I finally come face-to-face with the monster who's been haunting my dreams, the killer who has butchered so many women, and the murderous predator I've been hunting.

Cautiously, I leave the cover of the bushes and move forward again through the undergrowth, pushing aside low branches and weaving my way around tree trunks, navigating, in my mind's eye, toward the huge, imaginary red ring in the forest that I crudely drew as a small circle on the map.

Moments later, I catch sight of something through the gaps in the trees up ahead. A structure. Maybe a house, a cabin. I peer closer, then realize what it is. It's a log cabin nestled in a large clearing. There's a person standing on the porch, I'm certain of it, but I can't tell if it's a man or a woman. With careful steps, I move forward again, taking up position behind a wide tree trunk near the edge of the clearing.

When I look up again, the person is gone.

Excitement mixed with fear boils inside me.

It must be Pritchard; I tell myself this. He *is* here, using the empty cabin. From the angle where I'm positioned, however, I can't see all the clearing or anything that looks like the entrance to the fallout shelter that Frances described.

Five minutes pass with excruciating slowness while I decide what to do next. The sun has dipped below the treetops now, and I can't wait for the person I saw to emerge again. Darkness and coldness are seeping in all around me. I need to know. I need confirmation that it's really him.

Reaching down, I pick up a rock the size of a baseball and feel its weight. The cabin, with its tin roof, is no more than a hundred yards away. Stepping from behind the tree, I quickly creep to the edge of the clearing, lean back, then hurl the rock skyward.

Like a grenade following a parabolic arc, the rock curves across the air toward the cabin.

Then I tense. *Shit!* I've overthrown, put too much muscle into it. The rock is going to miss the roof. Suddenly, the rock plummets on its downward trajectory before hitting one side of the front gable with an almighty clang that rings out through the surrounding stillness.

I retreat behind the tree again.

I count off ten seconds. Then twenty seconds. I peer around the trunk.

Nothing. No movement. The porch is empty. Then the front door swings open and a person steps out.

A woman? Disappointment rapes my heart, leaving me feeling violated.

I was wrong. It wasn't Pritchard who I saw before. It was just some old, stout woman, late sixties perhaps, and overweight. From this distance I can just make out her gray hair, and...something else. Her face is bound in a white cloth, like a scarf. It looks odd, out of place. It's wrapped *around* her face, not across her head as I would expect a scarf to be.

The woman swivels her head side to side. Then she turns and looks straight at me.

I sink farther back into the trees and crouch down. Did she see me? I wait a full minute before looking up again.

The porch is empty. The woman is gone.

So much for Gus Tanner's cabin being empty. I can hardly blame Frances for the error. After all, she did say that she hadn't been up here in twenty years. Things change. Someone is obviously living in the place now.

Something is nagging at me, though, about the woman, and is holding me back from retracing my steps down to my car and finding a decent meal and a motel room for the night in town. I need to knock on the door of the cabin, ask the woman if there is perhaps another location in the foothills. It won't take long, and I'll make up some story about how I was thinking of renting this cabin, in case she asks me why I'm here.

Reaching the bottom of the porch stairs, I place my foot on the first step when the cabin door swings open violently, and the woman lumbers out to the top of the stairs. Even before I register what the object is she's holding in both hands, the familiar racking sound the object makes punches fear into my gut.

I see her face clearly now. She's not wearing a scarf. It's a heavy bandage that's wrapped around her face. Bloody drool is stringing down from her lips and her chin. Her cheeks look puffy, swollen, as though she's stuffed cotton wool inside them. Her eyes are wild with anger, and she's pointing a pump-action shotgun right at my face, with her finger on the trigger.

"Hold it right there, missy, less you want me to take your head clean off your shoulders."

26

THE VAULT

Emma floated in a milky half light, sandwiched between a ghostly gray bank of clouds above and a malevolent, oily blackness below.

She opened her eyes but couldn't see. The half light of her unconsciousness still lingered. Something covered her eyes, and someone had stuffed a cloth in her mouth. She gagged, trying to breathe, trying to get more air into her lungs. Her body felt boneless, and she couldn't move, like all her muscles had been sucked out from under her skin. Sensations were still there, and she could tell her wrists were bound tight, but her ankles felt unhindered.

Then the horror of her last memory burst into clarity. They had drugged her.

Fragments of recent memories, leftovers from the last moments of her consciousness, were all that she had. Further back—nothing. Looking forward—pure fear, thick and weighty, pressing down on her chest.

Shadows rippled across the haze in front of her eyes. Then there was that smell, a ghostly aroma she recognized. A young man spoke, his voice cold and clinical. "She's coming around. We'd better get started."

Get what started? Emma felt like she was an experiment, comatose and helpless on a life-sized pegboard, ready to be dissected, to be opened, and for her insides to be turned outside.

A young woman's voice this time, a mix of impatience and excitement. "Hold her legs. No, wider. Open them wider."

Emma tried to force her legs together, to counter what was happening, to force them shut. There was no response, however. She was a person very much alive, trapped inside a dead body. Yet she was aware of every sensation, especially touch, the sensitivity of every cell across her skin amplified a hundred-fold.

"Wider," the woman demanded.

Emma sensed her legs were now splayed wide apart, yet that wasn't what sent a shudder of horror coursing through her. It was the sensation she now felt making her realize she had no pants on and no underwear either.

"It's going to be okay." The woman again. Her hot, sour breath curled into Emma's ear, words designed to bait Emma into a false sense of complacency, disguising the sharp barb of terror hidden beneath. "You don't have to worry," the woman crooned. "Give in. Don't resist. It'll be much better for you."

Lies. All complete lies, and Emma knew it. While her body could offer no resistance at all against what was about to happen, her mind, the only weapon she now had full possession of, was going to fight tooth and nail to maintain her sanity. Her body would mend. Her mind? Maybe not. She couldn't scream, the gag rammed so deep into her mouth, and she was almost thankful that it was. At least one orifice out of three was blocked. Little comfort, but the tiniest fragment of comfort nonetheless.

A cold and hard object rubbed against the inside of one of her thighs, the sensation making Emma flinch in her mind, revulsion turning to horror, and she bit down harder on the gag.

"I said wider!" the woman snapped, all softness gone from her voice, replaced with a cruel determination.

Emma's hips felt like they were being pulled apart on some

medieval torture rack as powerful fingers dug into the tender insides of her knees. The tang of her own blood filled her mouth as the edge of her tongue burst bright with a stinging pain.

The cold, hard object moved higher up her thigh, closer, and closer toward where Emma would've given anything for it not to enter.

She forced out a muffled scream.

The woman's words in Emma's ear came again. "No one's going to hear you, bitch!"

A cold draft rippled across Emma's most sensitive parts. She was exposed, ripe, raw, as sensitive as a freshly cut wound.

Without warning, searing pain nuzzled into her. A dry, forced invasion of everything she held sacred. It continued for a moment, burying itself deeper. Then stalled. Then a forceful push, dragging inward the outer edges of her sensitive folds of skin.

Hot tears flooded Emma's eyes, dampness spreading behind her blindfold.

She tried to scream again but gave a choking whimper instead, the muscles in her neck corded tight, her teeth clenched. More blood filled her mouth.

"It's not working." The man's voice this time. "It won't go in any more. It's too big."

"It's not too fucking big!" the woman shrieked. "Here, give it to me."

More shadows danced across the insides of Emma's eyelids.

"You must corkscrew it in. Don't just thrust it in, you fucking idiot!" she berated. "Turn it as you push. See?"

The vile thing twisted into Emma, then began moving back and forth. Emma's insides sprang into a furnace of abrasive pain.

"This is boring," the woman declared moments later, and Emma felt the object withdraw.

The words that came next drove something far beyond horror

into Emma's mind. An all-crushing violation confirming that they wanted to truly vandalize her.

"Turn her over," the woman sneered. "Onto her stomach."

Out of the darkness, the man's voice. "Here, use some of this lubricant. It will help."

"No!" the woman hissed almost immediately. "I want her to suffer. I want her to feel it all. I want her to bleed."

Emma tried to blot out what came next, tried to block out the entire world of an invasion so brutal, so cruel, so unexpected, that her sanity almost imploded.

The pain that followed was so exquisite, so tearing, so alien, that for a while, Emma thought she had blacked out. Like a single neutron rammed into the very core of her nuclei, a chain reaction of excruciating, nerve-numbing agony began spreading between her buttocks, growing and growing until it engulfed her entire body. The infestation, the molestation, the indignity of it all numbed Emma's mind. And she escaped, ran away in her head, to a place as far as she could run. And when she reached that place, where a dark wall barred her further, she broke through it and kept running and running until the pain subsided, and she was reduced to a sobbing, bleeding mess on the cold tiled floor.

Alone, and surrounded by the atrocities, in her bruised and battered mind's eye, she stood up, then retreated a few steps, and imagined a door closing in front of her, on a vault buried deep inside her mind, sealing off everything that had just happened. Next, she spun the heavy combination lock, trapping the hideous memory inside before forcing herself to never remember the combination again.

Down this dark passageway, there were other doors. Doors she had created, rooms she had built, memories she had also trapped inside and had forgotten the combination to the locks. She had accumulated only a few over the past years of her young life. But this room, this vault that trapped her most recent and vilest memory of all, was by far the biggest, with the thickest door and the toughest lock to crack. For it imprisoned a monster so destructive that she knew if she ever allowed it to escape, allowed it a glimpse of sunlight, she may not have the strength or the courage to contain it again. It would consume her.

Curled up in a ball on the dusty cement floor, she whimpered, *"No more. It can't happen, it can't happen, it can't happen...again.*

Emma woke with a start and gasped. Musty air filled her lungs, and she sucked it in. She looked around. She was back in the room deep within the fallout shelter, her hands tied behind her back and ankles bound with the harsh rope again. The metal bed was still where she had dragged it. Someone had removed the toolbox. She rolled onto her side and took in the other side of the room.

The door was ajar. They would come back. This was just a prelude to the horrors still to come.

A fragment of her nightmare still lingered in her mind. But it wasn't a nightmare. It was a slither from her past. A cruel, vile reality not dreamed. Dolores and Pritchard were not the perpetrators of that memory. Others were. A memory that had jolted itself loose inside her head, causing the combination lock to the vault to momentarily spring open.

Now she could see the demon as it wrapped its clawed, skeletal fingers around the edge of the vault's thick door, searching, searching for her, searching to escape.

Emma sat upright.

It can't happen again.

27

MAZE

The logical thing for me to do is to hold my hands up like a perpetrator, and as unnatural as it is for me, I comply. "I'm sorry. I didn't mean to intrude."

The woman continues aiming the shotgun at my head, a dubious look on her face. I haven't had many guns pointed properly at me before because I've always drawn my weapon first and shot the other person dead.

The bottom half of the woman's face is definitely swollen, and I'm pretty sure that's an ice sling she's got wrapped around her head. Maybe she's got a broken jaw. My mind thinks about who might have hit her and why. Jealous husband? Cowardly boyfriend? Irate relative? I don't see any obvious facial injuries. No black eyes, broken nose or bruising. Did she get into a fight, and someone broke her jaw?

"This is private property," she states. Her fingers tighten around the weapon. "You're trespassing."

Gun-totin' Annie means business. She's holding a Mossberg 500 shotgun. It's smooth, reliable, one of the best shotguns you could buy for home defense. There's also a sidesaddle ammo rack attached to the butt, spare shells sitting in a snug little row in the loops. I'm taking the threat seriously. "I mean you no harm. I'm just looking for a friend of mine. Is this Gus Tanner's cabin?"

A flicker of indecision crosses her eyes, but the shotgun doesn't waver. "Who's asking?"

"My name is Carolyn Ryder. I work for the FBI." Well, I used to. She might just shoot me after all. "I'm looking for a missing young woman. Her name is Emma Block." I give the woman a quick verbal description of Emma.

Her hesitation grows, and this time the barrel of the shotgun dips a few inches. Now it's pointing at the middle of my throat. Cold comfort. If she pulls the trigger at this range, she will still obliterate everything from my neck up. For a split second, I see myself headless but still standing at the bottom of the stairs before toppling over.

"Perhaps you have seen her?" I ask. "Honestly, I'm just looking for this young woman who's gone missing. She's from Camilla."

More hesitation. The barrel drops a few inches more and a weirdly comforting notion comes over me; now she's aiming at my chest, I have a slightly better chance of surviving the blast there. Then to my surprise, and admiration, her aim moves diagonally to my left, and over my heart.

Damn!

"I have seen no young girl around here," she says. "It's just me living here alone. What do you want with her?"

"Like I said, she's gone missing. I'm just trying to help the family. Her mother has asked me to help find her."

At the mention of *mother*, her expression softens. A strand of bloody saliva drips from her mouth and down her chin.

Best for me to keep appealing to the woman's maternal side—if she has one, that is. "Maybe you know Karen Block? She lives in the town. Emma, her daughter, is her only child. She's just eighteen."

I watch the woman closely as more drool seeps from her mouth. The part of the bandage directly under her chin is sodden pinkish, and she looks like she's in a lot of pain. "Are you okay?" I ask.

When faced with a threatening situation from an unstable person, especially if that person is also pointing a shotgun at you, it's best to show some compassion, offer them help and understanding. Show that you care and that you don't want to harm them.

"Can I help you? I have medical training."

The butt of the shotgun is still pressed hard against her cheek and she's still aiming down the barrel at my heart. Yet her face has lost some of its menacing scrunch.

"Look, I'm happy to go. Leave you alone." It's an enormous gamble, takes balls, but I turn my back on her and begin walking away with my hands still raised. Hopefully, she is a clever woman, clever enough to know that if she shoots me in the back, then it's murder. No explanation to a DA or to a jury will save her in Georgia from a heart-stopping three-drug cocktail into her arm.

"Wait!" the woman calls out.

I stop and turn back to see the shotgun has been lowered. It dangles by the woman's side, making her look as though she has one really long arm. And her finger has come out of the trigger guard. Good. It worked. Now I can breathe normally.

"Look, I'm sorry," she says. "I live alone, and I don't take kindly to unannounced visitors. A few months back, someone tried to break into my home."

My home?

I lower my arms. "I was told that Gus Tanner's cabin hadn't been sold. I thought Emma, the girl I'm looking for, is maybe hiding out here because it's been empty for a while."

"Gus Tanner's cabin *hasn't* been sold," she corrects me.

Now I am confused. "Forgive me for asking, but you said that this was your home?"

The woman descends the porch steps and walks right to me.

I hold my ground.

She forces a smile as best she can, but it comes out more like a bloated grimace. She's definitely in a lot of pain, and I can see clearly now that it is indeed an ice pack that is wrapped around her face.

She gives me a weary look. "That's because this isn't Gus Tanner's old place."

I feel a punch in my chest. Not as bad as being hit with a shotgun slug, though. "Sorry, I must have gotten my wires crossed." More like I've blown an entire motherboard. "I was given directions by a woman who works in the diner at the gas station a few miles from here."

The woman smiles again, but this time she doesn't grimace. She points to her jaw. "If you were my dentist, then I would have shot you."

Okay. Sometimes I feel the same way.

"I'm sorry," she repeats. "I've just had my wisdom teeth removed, and my dentist told me I'd be fine. He gave me some painkillers. But they're not working. And the pain is a bitch." She pulls a handkerchief from her pocket that's all sodden with blood and saliva and wipes her mouth. "I must look like a sight. I've got to keep my jaw wrapped in this damn ice pack, but my gums keep bleeding on and off. My wisdom teeth have been fine for years, then one got infected. My dentist decided it would be better to get them all pulled."

I feel sorry for her, but not as sorry as I would have felt if she had shot me. She seems like a nice lady, living on her own, more than willing to defend her property. Who can blame her in the age that we currently live in. And I certainly didn't want to see her go down for the death penalty.

"I had my wisdom teeth out a few years back, and let me tell you it's no house party," I say. Without being asked, I step forward and as gently as possible, touch the sides of her jaw. She flinches, then gives me a nod. "The swelling will subside in a few more days," I say, feeling under her chin. "I guess your dentist was just trying to be optimistic." I finish with my amateurish but convincing examination.

"I wish he would have just told me the truth," she grumbles. "And I've nearly used up all the pills he gave me."

"Go easy on them. And keep the ice on it. It's the best thing you can do." I pause, looking around. "Is there anyone who can come up here with some more painkillers, deliver them to you?

She shakes her head and grimaces again. "Who was the woman who told you this was Gus Tanner's place?"

With all the swelling, the ice pack, and her drooling, the woman looks like she's been thrown under a bus. So, I may as well give her some company. "Her name is Frances. Like I said, she works at the gas station diner. She told me she hadn't been up here in a while."

The woman gives a slow shake of her head. "Frances Pridmore." She then gives what sounds like a wet, muffled chuckle. "I should've known. Frances got her directions wrong, but you can hardly blame her." Turning, she points over her shoulder, northeast. "Gus Tanner's place is about half a mile that way."

She turns back to me. "You took the left fork in the road when you should've taken the right one. The right fork takes you to Gus's place. It's about half a mile or so. But you'll have to backtrack to where the road splits and go right. There's no other road or walking trail that will get you directly there from here. Just badass bush."

"Thanks for the advice."

"And it is empty. Has been for years now. Some sort of legal wrangle between the family over back taxes. I try to keep an eye on it because I don't want kids up here vandalizing the place."

Now I feel foolish. "Frances also said that there's a fallout shelter on the property."

"Yeah," she says. "Gus was prepping for the end of the world. I've lived up here for over ten years, and he tried to convince me I should build a shelter for myself, too. He even offered to help. He had his own backhoe and everything. And for all those ten years, he tried getting into my pants."

Gus sounded like a genuine character. Maybe he used the fallout shelter as a means of foreplay, to cajole women up there so he could have his way with them. "Frances told me the same thing."

The woman rolls her eyes. "You're welcome to go up there, look around."

"You don't know if anyone has been up there recently?"

"I doubt it. But like I said, you're welcome to look."

I thank the woman and begin walking away. What little daylight is left is burning fast. Half a mile won't take me long. It's going to be almost dark by the time I get there, and I don't fancy poking around some old fallout shelter in the dark. The thought of it makes my skin crawl, and for the briefest of moments, the horrors of Utah come flooding back to me.

"Just be careful up there!" the woman calls out after me.

"I will."

"You don't understand. It's not just a fallout shelter."

I turn back and look at her.

"Gus was a crazy old bastard. He dug out nearly half the mountainside, creating a network of tunnels. God knows what's up there. Apparently, it's like a maze. But it's his land until it meets the southern border of the state forest that's about a mile north of his cabin. So, he did whatever he wanted to."

A maze of underground tunnels? Can my day get any worse?

"Oh, and another thing," the woman calls out. "I've seen a big pickup truck going along the road out front here a few times in the last couple of days. Haven't seen it around here before."

My skin fizzes with excitement. "Do you know what kind? Did you get a look at the license plate?" I know that's expecting too much.

"Not the plate. But it was black. A black RAM pickup truck."

Walking back, I take out my cell and call up the photo of the truck Vega pulled from the gas station security camera and show the woman.

She stares at the screen, then nods. "Yeah. That's the one. Thought it was maybe his family who live out of state or a developer looking to buy it."

"Are you positive it's the same truck as in the photo?"

"Yep. I used to own a Dodge RAM back in the day. My father drove them all his life, so I know them pretty well." She points at the photo on the screen. "That's one of the newer models, made after Dodge spun off RAM trucks into a separate division back in 2008. You won't see many of them like that one around here, let me tell you."

28

PANIC

Surely it must be Pritchard's. It's too much of a coincidence. Then again, it could be any number of black RAMs in the entire state. Well, no, not any number. Vega discovered there's over two thousand registered Dodge pickup owners, but as far as color? She couldn't drill down that far into that data.

Since I arrived, I've been scouring the traffic, keeping a lookout for that exact registration plate. But I've seen nothing so far. And now the woman said she saw it up here. Things are lining up, and yet I can't help but feel there's something missing, something obvious I can't see.

The trees thin, and I increase my pace, all the while keeping one eye on the dirt road on my right, using the cover of the tree line to shield me just in case a vehicle comes by.

My lungs are burning, but not as fierce as the flames raging inside me. It must be him. Pritchard is here. The light is fading, it's getting cooler, and sweat dribbles down my neck as I tick off a list in my head. Vega put him at the gas station, under a mile from where Emma Block's car was abandoned. We know the make and model and the license plate, too. And now we have a positive ID from a witness of the vehicle but not of Pritchard himself. Walter Pickford, the DMV registered owner of the truck, is an eighty-six percent photo match to Vega's facial-recognition software of how Pritchard now looks, based on the camera footage taken at the gas station. Pickford's DMV address, according to Vega, turned out to be nothing more than a vacant block on the side of the road five miles west of Peachtree City. Walter Pickford is an alias for Sam Pritchard.

The first stages of a game plan formulate in my head. I will not call local law enforcement if it is Pritchard. Aaron Wood will not be happy, but I don't care.

If the local cops get involved, like he has done many times before, Pritchard will slip away. I must confront him on my own terms. With no weapon and no backup, it's a risk. I know it. It doesn't worry me. I'll bash his brains in with a rock if I must, then leave his body for everyone to see. I want the world to know that he is dead.

With newfound determination, I press on harder, ignoring the weird feeling that something dark and malevolent is pulling me up the hillside. It's him, and he's sucking me toward him like a black ho—

I hear something behind me.

I pause and glance back. It's the sound of a vehicle coming up the dirt road. Quickly, I duck behind some thick foliage and peer out through the gaps. Moments later, the dirt road is lit by the headlights of a vehicle: a car not a pickup truck. I'm certain. The whine of a struggling engine, not the hungry, deep growl of a V8.

I relax slightly. Who else would come up here? Surely, it's not the woman I just spoke to, being nosy and all?

A car comes into view, driving slowly and cautiously up the dirt road. A four-door sedan, an old silver Ford Taurus, a woman behind the wheel. I can just make out her face, but I can't see her features clearly. The sedan slows as it approaches a curve in the dirt road, and for a moment it swings closer toward me. I push apart the branches of the bush to see better. The driver's side window is down, and I catch a glimpse of the woman's face. *What!*

Confusion hits me like a blow to the head, and my brain starts doing backflips.

No! No! No! It can't be.

The car takes the bend; the headlights sweep past me, and then it disappears out of sight around the curve farther up the road.

Why is she here? What is she doing? The answer hits me. Busting out from behind the bushes, I take off at a run, sprinting as fast as I can, chasing after the sedan.

Everything is going horribly wrong.

Shit! Shit! Shit!

DAMN! Damn! Damn!

Frances Pridmore cursed as she sat hunched behind the wheel of her faithful, old Ford Taurus.

Guilt, thick and heavy as a sumo wrestler, had sat on her as she painstakingly watched the clock inside the diner tick down until her shift was over thirty minutes ago.

It's all my fault, she thought. She had given the wrong directions to that woman. What was her name? Karen? No. Kirsty? No—Caroline. That was her name. Caroline.

Frances had told her to take the left fork along the dirt road when it should have been the right. And while she could just let it go, certain that Caroline, who seemed like a clever woman, would figure it out, the guilt kept weighing on her.

No. She had to do the right thing and drive up here after her shift and see if she could find her and apologize profusely. The last thing she wanted was for the woman to get lost in the woods, to be wandering around in the darkness.

Frances peered through the windshield, thinking to herself. It was the right thing to do, even if Caroline had taken the wrong fork in the road and had arrived at the property where Sally Rimes lived. Surely Sally would've pointed her in the right direction without too much fuss. That's why Frances had decided against driving first to Sally's place and go instead directly up to Gus Tanner's cabin, certain that Caroline would be there by now. Was someone being held up there against their will, as Caroline had suggested? If there was, then Frances was determined to find out. She had her cell phone on her and would call the police at the first sign of trouble.

Caroline reminded her of herself, a younger version, though. Fiercely independent, with a lot of get-up-and-go, someone who didn't seem to need a man around her all the time. Well, maybe that was a stretch. Frances didn't know the young woman that well.

As she drove on through the gloom, Frances made a mental note that she should call by Sally's place on the way back, just to see how the woman was doing. She liked Sally. A bit of a loner like her, self-sufficient, independent. Mind you, Frances hadn't seen her around town or in the diner for some time now.

I hope she's okay, she thought as she navigated around another bend in the dirt road.

It was getting dark really fast, and despite not being up here in ages, things still looked the same. Nothing seemed to change. Sure, the foliage along the sides of the road was more unruly, and there were a few more potholes than she could remember. But she had still found her way after all these years. Passing a bend a few moments ago, she was pretty sure she saw something on the left-hand side of the road in the beam of the headlights, just back in the trees. Maybe an animal was foraging around in the undergrowth.

Five minutes later, the Taurus crested the hill, and Frances drove into the clearing, and a log cabin came into view.

"What the hell?" Frances muttered as she hit the brakes.

The place was supposed to be unoccupied. Vacant. And yet as clear as day, in the beam of her headlights, she saw a black pickup truck sitting next to the cabin, three big letters emblazoned on the tail-gate: RAM.

Parking beside the truck, Frances climbed out, fighting words on her lips.

Whoever was here, in her mind, they were trespassing. She was certain of it. And she was going to give them hell.

29

DYING TWICE

Pritchard appeared in the doorway, a curious look on his face as he regarded Emma as she lay on the floor, her hands and feet tied.

His expression was different from Dolly's. It was still the look of a predator, but it glowed with a different kind of lust, a different kind of wanting, not the sexual cruelness Emma had seen in Dolly's eyes.

This was something else, and it worried Emma much, much more.

"She won't be long," he said, walking toward her. As he crouched down in front of her, she noticed, for the first time, the heavy black work boots he wore. They were scuffed and scarred, the leather skin of one toe slit open like a scalpel wound, part of the steel cap showing beneath. He didn't give Emma the slow, lecherous gaze over her body from head to toe, as Dolly had given every time the old witch cast her eyes on her. Instead, Pritchard had dark, pitiless eyes that seemed to claw into Emma's soul and never let go. He wore heavy work boots, scuffed and scarred, the leather skin of one toe slit open like a scalpel wound, part of the steel cap showing beneath.

"She's not going to kill you," he continued matter-of-factly.

His words seemed like an unfinished sentence derived from an unfinished thought inside his demented head, providing no comfort at all to Emma. It was all a lie. They were going to kill her. It was just a matter of whose face she would see before she gave her final gasp of breath.

Pritchard continued, his eyes never leaving hers. "It's not her thing. Killing."

Her thing? Emma knew perfectly well what Dolly's "thing" was and what was in store for her.

Pritchard tilted his head and for a moment appeared almost human. "And when she's had her way with you, then you'll be all mine."

The lack of emotion in his face drove complete certainty into Emma's heart together with his next words. "And you will die."

Despair, absolute and gut-wrenching, filled Emma.

"Let the fun and games begin," he said.

Then she watched as he stood and walked calmly out of the room.

For a few minutes, Emma lay on the floor, grappling with the unimaginable horrors that lay ahead for her. There was no false hope in Pritchard's words or in his demeanor. He meant what he had said. He wanted her to fully understand the hopelessness of her predicament. Not to prepare her, to give her a chance to accept her fate. Rather, it seemed like he wanted to instill deep-seated fear in her, as though it were a necessary part of his anticipated enjoyment. Her journey to certain death had already begun. He just wanted her to know it.

Emma fought against her bonds, but they were tied too tight. Her right hand and wrist ached from where Pritchard had nearly broken it when he disarmed her from the bread knife.

In frustration, she cried out.

She'd had her chance to escape, should've just taken off into the woods, not bothered about trying to find the keys to the pickup truck inside the log cabin. Instead, she had squandered it, frittered it away.

Now she had no chance at all at the hands of these two monsters.

First Dolly and then Pritchard. To endure one, just to die at the hands of the next.

It was like dying twice.

FRANCES CAUGHT sight of a small rectangle of light that was coming from the opposite side of the clearing, maybe a few hundred yards away. It was like a glowing rent in the darkness that drew her attention away from the log cabin. That must be the door to the fallout shelter, she thought. Someone was obviously down in the shelter, poking around, no doubt. Perhaps it was Caroline. She must have gone inside to look.

She turned back to the pickup truck that sat like a dark, silent beast hunkered down on its fat tires. She thought for a moment. Maybe she had jumped the gun earlier, assumed that it belonged to someone else who was trespassing on the property. Perhaps it was Caroline's ride? It just seemed like a strange type of vehicle for a woman to drive, though. Then she remembered how the woman had come across in the diner. Strong-willed, determined, slightly aggressive, but in an ambitious, not threatening way.

Maybe the pickup is hers after all?

She glanced at the cabin again. The windows were dark, and there were no signs of life. It must be empty. Caroline must have gone straight to the fallout shelter.

Frances looked back at the rectangle of light on the opposite side of the clearing, confusion slowly spreading in her mind.

If that were true, then how did she unlock the door? Surely the shelter had been padlocked or something?

The stars had come out, and a sliver of moon hung in the indigo sky. Frances stood her ground, unsure. Maybe she should get back in her car and leave. Caroline had obviously found the place and seemed fine. No. She had driven all this way to talk, to make sure the woman had found the place, and also to apologize. That was what she wanted to do. Say sorry for the mix-up.

Frances started toward the opening of the fallout shelter. Despite the warm glow of the moon above, and the knit cardigan she wore over her uniform, she couldn't shake the sudden prickle of coldness that had come over her.

30

SUBWAY SANDWICH

So wrapped up with despair and self-loathing, it took Emma several precious minutes before she noticed what was lying on the floor that wasn't there before Pritchard had entered the room.

The small red sausage-shaped object was no longer than her index finger. Shiny and bright red, it lay just a few feet away, directly behind where he had crouched down to deliver his death-row sermon to her.

Had he dropped it by accident? How could he have? She looked at the object with a mix of disbelief and bewilderment. Surely not?

With her ankles bound, and her hands tied securely behind her back, all she could do was flounder on the ground, like a helpless fish out of water. Yet, with one complete roll of her body, she managed to reach the object, her eyes inches from it. No, this wasn't on the floor before Pritchard entered. Something this obvious she would have noticed, especially on the bare cement floor.

Swallowing her confusion, she nudged it with her knee, then gasped. The small Swiss Army knife, or penknife was real, not an apparition conjured up by a last-ditch attempt at deluded optimism.

She quickly glanced up at the open door, almost expecting to see Pritchard striding back in, scooping up the knife and apologizing for being so reckless. And that was what plagued Emma as she shifted her focus back on the knife. He *wasn't* reckless. Dolly, perhaps, but not him.

Move, you doe-eyed bitch! the voice inside her head screamed, shaking Emma out of her trancelike state of amazement. *The fuckers will be back! Don't just sit there, you dumb shit! What the fuck are you waiting for?*

She wiggled her back over the knife, her fingers groping like the swaying tentacles of a sea anemone. "Come on! Come on!" she snarled through clenched teeth. Finally, her fingers closed around the knife, and she rolled herself up into a seated position.

Working her fingers, she found the small groove in the top of the main blade, prized it out and locked it into place, then dropped the knife.

Fuck!

She rolled onto the knife again, not caring if she cut herself picking it up. Blood was going to be spilled this time anyway, trying to escape. This much she knew.

Her fingers found the knife again, and she rolled back up to a seated position.

She glanced at the open door. *Were those footsteps?*

Relying purely on feel, she inverted the knife, then tried to force the sharp edge of the blade against the rope so she could start sawing through it.

Once, then twice, she fumbled and dropped the knife and had to start again.

On the third attempt, angry and frustrated, she slid the razor-sharp edge of the blade across the meaty part of her palm just below her thumb.

Blood, warm and slippery, began seeping from the cut, coating both her palms.

She glanced up at the door again. She needed to hurry. Dolly would be here soon, from which there would be no escape.

Ignoring the pain, she slowed her breathing, forcing her mind to focus. *You can do this! You know you can.*

She inverted the knife again and tried to find the rope with the sharp edge of the blade. But the angle was too tight, and when she found the rope with the blade, she couldn't exert enough downward pressure against the braids of the rope or move it back and forth enough to create a cut, and her fingers were now too slick and slippery with blood.

"No!" she hissed. Her anxiety ratcheted up another notch as the knife again slipped from her grasp. She had been given a second chance to escape, and now she was going to mess that up, too.

Find a way, Emma! her mind screamed. *Don't give up! That bitch witch is gonna be back soon. Then she's gonna fuck you seven ways to Sunday up the ass with that foot-long subway sandwich of hers before old bastard gramps slits your throat, leaving you to bleed out like a Thanksgiving turkey.*

"Shut the fuck up!" Emma snarled.

I can't! the voice squeaked. *If you die, then I die!*

"You don't think I already know that?" she murmured.

Emma took a deep breath, trying to calm the fear that was clawing up her throat like some hunched anime ghoul. Then she tried again.

It was no use. It was impossible to cut the tight rope and free her hands from behind her back using the small knife. The angle was too acute, and she was doing a better job of stabbing and slicing her palms than she was cutting through the thick, coarse rope. Her feet were bound tightly, too, and she couldn't exactly hop her way to freedom like some bunny rabbit.

There must be a better way. She just needed to...run?

Run?

Of course!

"You dumb ass!" Emma cursed herself for the precious minutes she had wasted. The answer was obvious.

Years of practicing Jujitsu had given her the flexibility to contort and twist her limbs into all manner of shapes and angles to maneuver and untangle herself from the clutches of a persistent opponent.

Quickly, she sat on her hands, then wiggled her buttocks over them before bringing her arms forward on either side of her hips. Her hands cleared her buttocks. With them under her thighs, she tucked her knees up tight to her chest until the backs of her heels touched her fingers. Holding her breath, she hunkered into as tight a ball as she could, then pulled her legs through her arms and her feet over her bound wrists.

Now her bound hands were in front of her, not behind her back.

Without wasting a second, she snatched up the knife and began attacking the rope around her ankles. With her hands in front, she could see where to cut and could exert more downward force on the stout cord.

Yes! The edge of the blade sank into the rope, releasing curly twists of fiber as it went back and forth. Emma checked the door again but kept the blade moving feverishly back and forth. In her mind's eye, she could almost see Dolly waddling down the steps of the tunnel toward her, reaching the bottom, then coming along the narrow passageway.

The voice inside her head had come back. *Cut faster! Otherwise, Dolly and her enormous dildo will catch you!*

Emma turned her attention back to the rope.

Within seconds, she cut through the first coil of rope, then the next one below, and then finally the last coil.

Her ankles were free!

Folding back the blade, Emma slipped the Swiss Army knife into the front pocket of her shorts, then bolted for the door.

The passageway outside was empty.

She started running, running for her life, her life that she thought was going to be snuffed out in a matter of minutes from now. She had been given a second chance, and she knew there wouldn't be a third.

Someone was looking out for her. A guardian angel.

31

FINITO

The sound of the car fades, and somewhere up ahead above the treetops, I can see a dull sliver of moon rising.

I run faster. Frances cannot reach the cabin first if Pritchard is there. He will surely kill her, and it will be my fault. She's a kind soul, a genuinely nice person who is only trying to help. Obviously, she must have realized she had given me the wrong directions. Instead of leaving me to my own devices to find the correct cabin, she's driven up here to find me. It's not her fault, but if she dies, I will never forgive myself.

I'm on the dirt road, out in the open, but I don't care who sees me now. Getting to the cabin as fast as I can is my only concern. I've jettisoned my backpack containing my water and a flashlight, so I can run faster. I stumble several times, my toes catching on large stones, my ankle jolting as my foot suddenly skews into a pothole. The road is rutted and furrowed, uneven and callous on my feet. My heart is pounding, and I ignore the burning sensation in my thighs, calves, and throat.

It can't be that much farther now surely. The road flattens out, and I increase my speed as it curves to the left before cutting through a gap in the hedge. I keep running hard.

Silhouettes of trees crowding around me. A canopy of branches thickening over me like earth being tossed over my coffin, trapping me inside.

Moments later, I emerge into an expanse of open ground, a cabin on the right, and immediately my gaze is wrenched to an oval glow in the distant darkness on my left. It's as though someone has cut a hole into the black fabric of the night and is shining a search beam through it.

With my chest heaving and my lungs screaming, I skid to a halt to catch my breath.

The luminous opening is just hanging there in the darkness, and as mesmerizing as it is, something urges my eyes back to the cabin on the right. Then the devil touches my soul as my eyes find what is parked next to it. The cabin is in darkness, but there's enough moonlight to give the skin of a black RAM truck a ghostly pale sheen. Shadow obscures the license plate, yet my intuition is clear and unhindered.

Automatically, I reach for my handgun—to find there's nothing on my waist, just my belt.

The Ford Taurus I saw before is parked next to the pickup truck and I rush to it, but there's no one inside. Then I catch sight of the license plate on the truck, and it's like my stomach has fallen all the way to my aching feet.

Pritchard is here. It's his truck.

But where is Frances? Where did she go?

I angle around to the front of the cabin just in time to see the door open and a person emerge from the shadows. Is that a gun in their hand? Then my face is flooded with light. The person is shining a flashlight on me.

Raising my hand, I try to make out their features.

Then a voice I don't recognize. A woman.

"Who the fuck are you?"

I can't see her face, just a dark cutout behind the corona of the flashlight. But I can tell from the tone that she's not a friend, but a foe.

Then another voice from behind me. A voice that makes my blood curdle.

"She was FBI," he says. "And this time I am going to kill her."

I turn to see Sam Pritchard standing behind me. A bear of a man with all the stealth of a silent, slithering python, with stone-cold killer eyes. Yet, I see something else in those eyes. The smiling faces of dead women. Their living reflection trapped forever in his irises, as though seeing my own reflection as they had all once, standing in front of him, a heartbeat away from death.

What I'd give right now to have that sweet Mossberg pump-action in my hands that the woman I had met before had pointed at me when I had taken the wrong turn. I'd cut the bastard in half, then quarters, then eighths, and keep shooting until he was just a wispy, bloody cloud of vapor.

"FBI!" the woman on the porch behind me screeches.

I ignore her. She falls away from my attention because everything now, my entire world, is focused on just Pritchard. Nothing else matters. I may be standing in the middle of a moonlit field, under a billion stars, surrounded by thousands of chirping insects in the spring evening air, on a planet that's slowly turning with billions of people, yet it feels like we're the only two people left in the entire universe. All life, everything, seems to have suddenly been sucked into the vortex that he spins around himself. His presence is so dark, so malevolent that it distorts my reality. But it is really him this time, not an illusion. Rotten flesh and poisoned blood, he is not of this world.

Moonlight glistens off his dark orbs. Like invisible tentacles, his hatred for me, I can feel slithering around my throat, my waist, my breasts, my soul. For some inexplicable reason, I feel drawn to him. This is the first real chance I've had to take a good, long, hard look at him up close. Not a fleeting glimpse out of the corner of my eye as he vanishes wraithlike down a mine shaft or into a cave.

"Caroline!"

I hear a name being called. Not mine, but it's for me. Breaking my trancelike state from Pritchard's eyes, I turn toward the voice I recognize. Now the fear comes, viscous and suffocating, it fills up the hollows of my lungs.

"Caroline! There you are." The voice is soft and inquisitive.

The beam of the flashlight jerks away from me and sweeps toward Frances Pridmore, who is approaching our little Mexican standoff from around the side of the log cabin, her cell phone lighting her face.

She stops when she sees that I'm not alone.

The flashlight beam finds her face, and she raises her hand to block the glare. "What's going on? Who are you people?"

Through the gaps between her fingers, she stares at me. "Caroline, what's happening? Do you know these people?"

"It's *Car-o-lyn*, not *Car-o-line*," Pritchard drawls, his devil's tongue edged with sarcasm. My name on his tongue makes me feel like he's just taken a long, wet lick up my naked spine.

Keeping the beam of her flashlight on Frances, the woman on the porch descends the stairs, the old wood creaking in protest as she does. She is bulky, squat, almost apelike.

I need to move. My mind scrolls through a limited set of options —all offering varying degrees of bad to totally diabolical. Picking one in the next few seconds is unavoidable, otherwise I'm going to die and so is Frances.

In a heartbeat, I map out the only plausible scenario. A threat behind me, a predator directly in front of me, and an innocent bystander to my right. While I'm not armed, the woman, judging from her build, is likely to be. Pritchard prefers his bare hands.

There is no other viable option.

I blink and see faces staring at me from the wall in my small basement office. Is this what they last saw? Pritchard's dead eyes? A portal to their impending afterlife of nothingness?

I'm going to die anyway, and for me, there is no afterlife. Just "before death," then nothing. You just cease to exist. No nirvana. No pearly gates. Your internal hard drive gets wiped, then finito.

I think of the colors of the leaves in the fall in Vermont, New Hampshire, and in the Berkshires. That's where I want to be when I die. To see the carpet of color, the change of seasons, all the beauty and majesty, to be surrounded by a kaleidoscope of gold, okra, burnt orange, bronze, copper, and rust red.

Not here. Now it appears the choice has been snatched from me, and that makes me really mad. Where I die will not be a place of my choosing. It will be here, on this very earth I'm standing upon.

"Run Frances! Run!" I scream.

Then I turn and lunge at Pritchard.

32

DROWNING

At the last moment, I peel away from Pritchard because my dumb emotions get the better of me, torn between my urge to kill him and my unwavering need to save the innocent.

It's Frances I need to protect. I don't know who the woman is with the flashlight, but Pritchard will kill Frances if she gets in his way.

The woman with the flashlight, despite her short, stocky, and overweight build, is moving toward Frances with incredible speed. I keep running, then crash into the woman just as she's reaching out toward Frances, the glint of a knife in her other hand. We hit the dirt together, and I drop my elbow into the side of her head with a sickening crunch. The woman snorts like a pig, then bucks me off. I roll away and come up in a ready crouch to see Frances, statue-like, her face twisted in horror, staring down at the knife in the woman's hand.

"Run!" I scream at Frances again, but it's like I'm screaming at Lot's wife. Instead of a pillar of salt, Frances has turned into a pillar of ice, frozen solid to the ground.

The woman I elbowed in the head is squirming and moaning in the dirt. Temporarily dazed by my blow, she's now coming to her senses.

To my left, Pritchard is walking slowly toward us like he's got all the time in Texas. He's going to kill Frances, then me. He wants me to witness her death first. He's going to taunt me, keep her alive for a few minutes so I can then watch him kill her slowly in front of my eyes and then blame me for her death.

I spring off the ground, kicking the knife from the woman's grasp. It scuttles into the darkness. Then I kick her in the head. A brutal, lights-out blow, as I pass her before heading for Frances.

Pritchard reaches Frances first. A lamb to the slaughter. He has no weapon. His meaty hands are enough. He's wrapped them plenty of times around the throats of women before snapping their necks.

Rage tears at my insides as I barrel into Pritchard. It's like hitting a football tackle bag that's filled with rocks, not foam. Pain explodes in my right shoulder, and I literally ricochet off him like a pinball, then tumble to the dirt.

On my back, I see him looking down at me. My effort was a distraction at best, but I'll take it if it means drawing him away from Frances.

Ignoring Frances for the moment, he reaches down and clamps one hand around my throat, then lifts me until I'm on my tiptoes. He turns my head one way, then the next, appraising me like some predator that fell from outer space into the jungle. Dark eyes smother me, and I can barely breathe.

Then looking over his shoulder, I catch a glimpse, Frances.

Finally, she's moving, backing away. I can't see the woman on the ground, but I imagine my kick to the head has rendered her unconscious.

Then the punch comes, as I knew it would. A driving fist into my stomach. Now I know what it feels like to be a winter sweater in spring, being placed inside one of those plastic vacuum bags, having all the air sucked out of you.

Pritchard drops me to the ground, and like Alice in Wonderland, I feel myself shrinking in size, my body deflating itself of all air from the vicious punch.

Looking up at the stars, I silently gasp at the infinite quantity of air above me, unable to draw in a single breath. I know the feeling will pass, and I also know by then, Frances and I will probably be dead.

Rolling on my side, I catch a glimpse of a flickering light in the distance and realize I'm looking at the lit opening of the fallout shelter. I blink hard. It's not an apparition. I see her, her body framed by the glowing aperture. It's Emma, I'm certain of it. Her silhouette stands motionless for the briefest of seconds before running off, her hands down, toward the woods.

I blink, and she's gone.

My lungs still won't work, won't inflate, and my oxygen-starved brain is screaming at me.

As a kid, I remember my father taking me to the local swimming pool. I couldn't swim, so I clung to the side while he explained to me how to dog paddle. Then a friend of his walked past, and he was distracted, began talking to him. I don't know how it happened, but my fingers slipped, and I sank to the bottom of the pool right beside my father's feet. Strangely, surrounded by the watery silence, I felt at peace, calm. No hint of panic entered my adolescent brain. I held my breath for what felt like two minutes and then tugged on my father's knee. He then promptly lifted me out, apologizing profusely. After, he bought me an ice cream. I knew it was a bribe. I might have been a kid, but I wasn't stupid. So, I didn't tell Mom what had happened. But from that day on, I had conditioned myself for moments in my life when I would be unable to breathe, either through fear or because someone was strangling the shit out of me. I learned to remain calm, composed, despite the screaming in my head, and problem-solve my way out of a dangerous situation. I became good at not needing to breathe, assessing the situation, and then reacting, moving, taking action.

At least Emma is safe. With a fire raging inside me that doesn't need oxygen, I roll up to my feet, and then my world collapses.

Pritchard is standing a few feet away, the body of Frances limp like a rag doll in his huge hands. Her neck is bent at an acute angle, the side of her face touching the top of one shoulder.

A high-pitched whistle fills my ears and my head throbs. I can't hear myself scream, but I can feel my jaw ache as my mouth goes wide, my teeth bared. Air floods into my lungs.

Pritchard turns toward me, Frances still held in his grip. It's almost like he is offering her to me as a sacrifice. A dead bird whose neck he has just broken.

He releases her, and she falls in a heap, like a pile of empty clothing.

Then he, the devil's only true disciple on earth, smiles at me, tempting me, goading me to act, to do something.

33

RUN, RABBIT, RUN

Run, Emma. Run, Emma. Run! Run! Run! Dolly's going to stick her dildo up your bum! bum! bum!

Tearing through the dark woods, Emma could not get the song lyrics, the imagery, and the shock of it all out of her head. Driving with her mom through town one day when she was a kid, the "golden oldie"—as described by the radio jock—had come on WMTM 93, the local station. There was something both comical and morbidly disturbing about the crackling vinyl tune that had stuck in Emma's adolescent head. Now the little voice inside her head had adapted the lyrics to match the horrifying predicament she found herself in. The image of Dolly, not a farmer, a massive dildo, not a gun, and her bounding away like a startled rabbit had given Emma enough impetus to keep running, to put as much distance as she could between her and the two crazies.

All sense of distance, direction, perspective, such as background and foreground were distorted by the shadowy charcoals and grays that surrounded her as she ran. One thing wasn't distorted, however. Her fate—if they caught her—would come brutally and swiftly. There would be no third chance, no dragging her back to that creepy underground dungeon and tying her up again. They would kill her where they caught her. Hang her from the nearest tree even, like a... dead rabbit.

Run, Emma. Run, Emma. Run, run, run! The ominous words with the spritely, carefree melody filled her head again, forcing her to run faster, her bound hands bobbing in front of her like she was conducting some maniacal orchestra.

And they *were* chasing her. She had no doubt. Like a thick blackness driving at her from behind, she could feel them. *Satan's hounds.* Yes, she thought. That was a better description of those two fuckers. The man especially. Dolly was just as vile and as disgusting, but there was something more disturbing, more unhinged about the man. His eyes, for one. Looking into them made Emma feel like she was leaning over the stone lip of a medieval well, peering into the darkness below, only to discover a bottom chock-full of dead kittens.

He had a suppressed determination, a restrained confidence about him that was far more disturbing than the piglike hunger of the woman. She was rudimentary, guttural, blatant about her vile intentions for Emma.

The man, he seemed to linger more in the background, watching with those dead eyes. He was the quiet one. Biding his time until she became his. That was what he had told Emma. *Then you'll be all mine.*

She stumbled, catching her ankle on something, and fell hard.

Fuck!

She rolled up into a sitting position, her hair speckled with leaves and twigs, and looked back to where she had come, expecting to see the bobbing of flashlights behind her. The woods were silent, unmoving. She checked her ankle. It seemed uninjured, no sprain, thankfully. Gathering herself up, she started off again, at a slower pace this time, glancing over her shoulder now and then just to make sure.

Through the gaps in branches above, pale moonlight filtered down, partially lighting the way. She would stop soon, take a moment to use the knife differently to cut the ropes around her wrists. Maybe hold the knife between her knees and saw through them that way.

Until then, she wanted to put as much distance as she could between her and the others.

Others? In her haste to flee, Emma had almost forgotten. Someone was holding a flashlight, and she was certain she had seen another person standing there. Emma had only paused at the entrance to the fallout shelter for a few seconds just to get her bearings again. She was certain she had seen three people in the clearing in front of the log cabin. No doubt another accomplice of the other two, Emma thought. Invited to join in the sick party where she was the special guest of honor.

After ten minutes, Emma slowed from a jog to a brisk walk before stopping near a rocky formation where she could hide behind for a while. She turned and glanced into the woods behind her that were full of muted shapes and crooked angles. She saw no movement. It was a temporary reprieve that she intended to use.

Under the cover of the rock formation, she reached for the penknife in her pocket. The blood had dried on it and wasn't as slippery. However, it was the same problem as before. Even with the knife held between her knees, it kept slipping. It was impossible to create any decent pressure in the blade to cut through even just a few strands of the rope without the knife moving.

Her heart sank. It was impossible.

It was all made-for-television bullshit, where the hero was able to easily cut through ropes around their wrists with a knife, she thought. Television villains were either dumb or really bad at tying ropes and knots. The man who had tied her up was neither.

Pivoting around the rocks, she looked back from where she had come. No one was there, but they were coming. It would just be a matter of time, and Emma needed to get her hands free, otherwise she wouldn't stand a chance of fighting them off.

She cursed, forcing back tears. No, she would not cry, she told herself.

Then the voice inside her head, the same one as before spoke up.

Find a way, Emma! There's always a way. Rabbits have big sharp teeth, don't they? Like beavers, if you ask me.

Bringing her hands up, she began biting, then tearing with her front teeth at the knots. Spirals of fiber started to come away, and she spat them out of her mouth and continued attacking the rope with her teeth, refusing to be trapped in a rope snare like a wild animal.

She paused, a few rope fibers clinging to her front teeth.

Trapped? A trap?

Her mind cut back to when she first noticed the penknife on the floor. Was it a trap? Why? Another test maybe? She thought about the toolbox that had been on the floor in the room when she awoke from being drugged and how odd it looked. Was that a test as well? Had the man deliberately dropped it? He seemed more meticulous, more guarded, more conscious of what he was doing than the woman, Dolly.

He didn't seem like the type of person who would make mistakes and certainly not as big a mistake as dropping something as useful as that in front of a woman he had just bound with rope.

Emma felt her insides twist as she realized.

It's a game for him, like a cat tormenting an injured mouse. Not killing it right away, but playing with it, drawing out the enjoyment for as long as possible. She shivered. He truly was a predator, and now he was hunting her. He had deliberately dropped the knife because he wanted her to escape, so he could give chase. For him, it was all about the hunt, not the kill. Dolly got her sick thrills via more barbaric means. While the man, Pritchard, as she had called him, had more sophisticated tastes.

He was coming after her, hunting her. That was what he had wanted to do all along, but Dolly thwarted his plans.

With renewed vigor, Emma attacked the rope with her teeth, chewing, pulling, and spitting out strands. It felt like her teeth were being wrenched from her gums, but she kept going. Then a loop of one of the knots loosened, a small gap appearing within the twists of the knot. Seeing this, Emma chewed and pulled like a starving animal ripping flesh from a carcass. The knot began to unravel, until eventually Emma could pull her wrists apart and unwind the rope.

She was free, at last.

Picking up the rope, she hurled it triumphantly into the trees. Then the singsong melody started up again inside her head.

Run, Emma. Run, Emma. Run! Run! Run!

34

TWO IS ONE

There is something innately horrible about someone killing another human being with their bare hands.

A bullet or a knife, most times, leads to a gradual passing of life. Even if it takes just a few seconds for a person's breath to slow, stutter, then eventually stop, it's a progression toward an eventual death. But seeing the listless body of Frances, with all her life snuffed out in the blink of an eye with a quick snap of the neck, is something truly awful that I will never forget.

Looking down at the body of Frances, I feel ultimate disbelief. How? She was alive just moments ago. How can life end so quickly, so suddenly as though a switch can get flipped—and bang! You're nothing? Gone, not even a memory yet because memories of the person haven't had enough time to form properly in your mind because it is that soon and that sudden. She is dead because of me, even though I didn't kill her. I am to blame for the collateral pain and suffering that will surely ensue with her family and friends all because of me.

Pritchard is standing like Frankenstein, watching me, a hideous, twisted smile of enjoyment on his face. That he has said nothing to me is even more disturbing. If I had my trusty Glock by my side, I'd put the entire magazine into his grinning face, reload, and then do the same to the woman. I'd probably end up in jail for using excessive force.

Memento mori. Remember, you must die.

As bad as I feel right now, I must regain my focus. Frances is gone, reduced to a lifeless heap in front of me. No amount of further screaming will change that fact. Swallowing, I compartmentalize the anguish I'm feeling, forcing it into a box that I will open another time to lament over. Now is not the time or the place. I must give Emma every fighting chance I can. And if that means doing a dance of death with the devil himself and one of his minions, for as long as possible, then so be it.

Like some grotesque zombie, the woman first gets to her knees, then staggers to her feet and produces a knife. Another knife? A slick little switchblade that clicks when she opens it. She's just full of surprises.

They circle me, Pritchard to my left, the woman to my right. Her face alternates between moonlight and shadow as she moves. Now I can see her busted jaw. Skewed and swollen, it makes her head look like a balloon. Maybe my aim was off. I thought I kicked her higher around the temple. A thick, silvery scar runs from one corner of her mouth, that adds to her warped, deranged look.

Keeping an eye on both, I join in the dance as well, circling back to my right, to where the woman is. She's the weakest, the injured party, and couldn't have fully recovered yet. Taking her out first, permanently, is a no-brainer for a woman whose demented brain is probably still wobbling inside her skull like a plate of Jell-O.

As if sensing my plan, Pritchard steps in, blocking the woman. "No," he says in a calm, even voice. "She's mine. You had the girl. I allowed it. But she's mine."

Well, that certainly clears up any ambiguity.

The woman goes to open her mouth, but Pritchard turns and throws her a look that I imagine could peel all the skin from her face.

She closes her mouth, but that doesn't stop her eyes burning pure hatred at me.

Pritchard turns back to me. "Ex-FBI Agent Ryder," he says. "It's been a while."

I don't know what's worse, him remembering me or that he knows I'm no longer in the FBI. As I have been following him, it now dawns on me he's also been keeping tabs on me.

"Let the girl go," I say. "Don't go after her."

He smiles, and I catch a glimpse of his sharp little teeth, the same teeth he sank thirty-six times into Barbara Weyland, nineteen, a sophomore studying law at the University of Missouri, Kansas City. Right now, she's staring at me from the wall in my basement office, pleading with me to kill him in the worst way possible.

"The cunt escaped again?" the woman croaks, blood dribbling down her chin like a feasting vampire.

"I know," Pritchard replies, his eyes never leaving mine. "I saw her just a moment ago running from the entrance of the shelter." He licks his lips, seemingly calm. "We'll catch her. She won't get far."

In the darkest depths of my heart, I know what he is saying is true. He has a reputation to uphold after all. No survivors. No one gets away. A clean sheet. Only ticks, no crosses.

Against all my beliefs, an idea springs to mind. It's based on an adage, a time-honored principle that's been tested countless times before.

Two is one. One is none.

Being prepared and all that Boy Scout stuff. I kind of like to think of it as two guns are better than one. I wrestle with this new idea, flipping and flopping it around inside my head. I don't like it, but right now it's the only thing that makes sense in the totally senseless hell I'm in.

Without wasting any more bandwidth on the decision, I turn and do what I hate doing. I run, sprinting toward where my best guess is as to where Emma plunged into the woods and vanished. She's all alone, and Pritchard and his demented minion are going to go after her no matter what.

And if she's going to survive, then she's better off with me than without me.

Two *are* better than one.

35

ENTRAILS

For the last twenty minutes, I've been wrestling with whether or not this is a good or bad idea.

Should I have tried and killed Pritchard there and then while I had the chance? And what about the old woman? His accomplice? As much as I'd like to think I am capable, without a gun, the odds were stacked against me. I'd be dead right now, lying next to Frances, and Emma would be left to fend for herself.

No. It was the right choice, even if it burns me like acid inside to think that I actually ran like a dog with its tail between its legs. Well, I know that's not exactly what happened. There was no cowardice in the act. Just probability.

The trees close in around me, but there's enough ambient moonlight to guide me. The plan is to stick to a straight line. I'm hoping, in her panic, that's exactly what Emma did. Most people, when they flee from danger, naturally run in a straight line, trying to put as much distance between them and the threat as they can. It's not something we do consciously as humans. More likely, it was instilled into our cerebral cortex the first time someone turned and ran from a woolly mammoth or a saber-toothed tiger.

I'm assuming that's what Emma has done, barring some insurmountable obstacle like a cliff or a mountain or a raging river that could get in her way.

Pritchard and the woman are going after Emma. I know that in my heart, that and the fact that when I first entered the woods, I looked to see if they were following me. They weren't. I watched moments later, as the RAM pickup truck roared to life, then tore out of the place, lights blazing before the sound of the throaty V8 faded into the distance. They weren't making a run for it either. No one is escaping Pritchard. No one. There must be other dirt tracks throughout the woods that he knows about.

I pause and get my bearings. I think I'm following a straight line. But I can't be certain. It's ironic that Emma is probably running from me now as well, even though I'm trying to save her, not kill her. I've got nothing with me except my cell phone, and I've got plenty of signal, too. It would be all too easy just to call the police, call in the cavalry, so to speak. They'll set up roadblocks, cordon off the area. And yet, despite all of that, I know Pritchard will slip through and escape as he has done before.

I much prefer being on my own. It's just me, Pritchard, and Emma now—and that woman. It's strange because he's never had a partner before. It's always been just him, by himself.

Slipping out my cell, I glance at the screen. It's so tempting, but that's not how it's going to go down. I pocket it and head off again. Perhaps I'm being too selfish. Perhaps it's my ego. Maybe it is. Maybe I just want to catch Pritchard on my own.

As I move, my eyes scan the darkness. I don't mind the dark as I'm aboveground, which is a blessing. But I don't think I could've gone down into that fallout shelter if I had to. I'm just afraid of being underground, buried in a tomb, tons of earth above me. I keep moving, checking the position of the moon every so often, keeping my ears peeled for the faint sound of Pritchard's truck. He must know another way in, and if I stumble across another dirt road, I may have to follow it.

Then a cold pocket of air hits me, and I stop stock-still, only my eyes moving. Something skitters in the undergrowth in front of me, maybe an animal. Without warning comes a cry, a high-pitched scream that cuts through the darkness, sending my skin crawling with a million ants. The scream chokes off to an eerie silence, and everything around me goes still.

Then the clouds part across the moon, bathing everything around in a cold, insipid light. There, maybe fifty feet ahead of me, I see something.

Emma?

Is it her? Was it a scream I just heard?

Shapes slither over each other in my vision, making me dizzy. I totter forward, then stop when the thing I saw moments ago begins to grow and swell. A wave of nausea creeps over me, and I steady myself against a tree.

Please, not now, I pray. I don't need this right now.

Swallowing, I shut my eyes. Not now. Please.

Then I open them again, to the sight and sound of something moving away from me in the foliage ahead. I wait a few minutes until it is gone, then I walk slowly toward where I saw it.

The sweet smell of blood hits me before I see the ripped-open carcass of a white-tailed deer, a wide rent in its soft underbelly, a string of glistening entrails protruding from within. I must have scared off whatever killed the deer. Seems like Pritchard isn't the only predator I may have to contend with.

Then a sound rides the slight breeze. A distant echoing, like an animal but hollow. My eyes scan the woods around me as I try to pinpoint the direction. The sound changes pitch, gears shifting down, then shifting up.

A truck. It is Pritchard. It has to be.

I start running.

36

UNHAPPY CAMPERS

Emma stumbled into the clearing, her eyes casting about.

A small log fire, a tent, camp table and chairs, the smell of meat cooking. It was a warm and welcoming sight.

Hunched around the camp table were a man and a young girl, a child with strawberry-blonde curls. He was perhaps in his mid-thirties. She was no older than six.

They both turned in unison and stared at Emma as though she were some kind of yeti emerging from the wilds.

The man stood while the girl remained seated, regarding Emma with wide-eyed wonderment. The young girl didn't look frightened, but a mild suspicion of Emma grew on her face as she watched on. The man, however, seemed more measured, practical in his assessment of Emma.

Emma slowed her breathing and imagined what she must have looked like to the pair, her hair nested with twigs and leaves and matted with sweat, fingernails black with dirt, shins banged up and bleeding, scratches along her arms, knees scuffed, her face a mask of grime and desperation.

"Sorry," she said, her mind racing for a plausible explanation that would not scare the both of them. The young girl had the same inquisitive brown eyes as the man. "I was out hiking and got lost," Emma said.

The man's expression softened slightly. The young girl remained dubious about Emma.

"Oh," he said, seemingly lost for words.

She stepped forward and felt the warmth radiating from the small campfire on her skin, feeding heat into her chilled bones. It might have been spring, but the woods were cold and unforgiving.

Two steaks were cooking on the grill, dripping fat into the hot coals beneath, which sizzled and spat. Her stomach rumbled with sudden hunger at the sight and smell. She pushed aside her craving for food and water. "Do you have a cell phone I can use?"

The man hesitated, indecision in his eyes. He turned to the girl, then back to Emma. "Sorry, I don't," he replied.

The young girl stood and moved next to the man, clinging to his thigh, her suspicious eyes focused on Emma.

The man patted the top of her head. "It's okay, Casey. This young woman is just lost. Nothing to worry about." He smiled at Emma. "How long have you been in the woods for?"

"I'm not sure. I was hiking and got lost. Lost my phone, too. I slipped and fell." At least that would explain the state I'm in, Emma thought.

"I'm Jack, by the way. And this is my daughter, Casey." He glanced down at the young girl.

Emma forced a smile and could feel herself growing impatient. Any moment now, she expected the man to produce a guitar, and they would all settle in around the campfire and start singing "Kumbaya" and toasting marshmallows. She needed a cell phone. She needed to call the police, get them here as soon as possible.

She glanced over her shoulder, back into the thick wall of darkness where she had emerged from. She felt safe for the moment. There had been no sign of them. Turning back to the father and daughter, Emma saw that the man's expression had changed slightly.

"Is everything okay?" he asked, his eyes looking past her to where she had glanced.

No. There's two, possibly three, fucking psychos chasing me. "I'm fine," Emma answered, turning down the volume of the little voice inside her head that had returned. She had to play it cool, not panic and scare the little girl or the father. Otherwise, who knows how they would react, especially the girl. She could start screaming and everyone within a mile would hear.

The man shuffled awkwardly. "Look, I wish I had a cell phone. But this is a father-and-daughter trip. Spending quality time together without the distractions of work and home."

The young girl looked up at her father. "That's right, Daddy. No distractions. No work."

Emma glanced past them to the small camp table where a pink Barbie tea set sat.

The man gave Emma a sheepish grin. "It's the first break I've had in a long time, with work and everything."

"And it's just the two of you?"

"My wife is pregnant with our second. She's at home. Her sister is visiting." He pulled the girl closer to his leg. "I wanted to spend some time with just Casey before the new baby arrives."

Emma understood. She had never experienced father-and-daughter time and was slightly envious of the hokey Hallmark moment that was unfolding before her. Yet it seemed so absurd. Who the hell goes into the wilderness, especially with a young child, and not carry a cell phone with them? What happened if one of them got injured? Got bitten by a snake or attacked by a bear? How would they call for help?

"Do you have any water?" That was the second priority on her list. In her head she already put a big red cross next to *Cell Phone.*

"Shit!" the man swore.

"Daddy!" the girl moaned, looking up at her father. "Mommy said you cuss too much! That's another dollar in the cussing jar."

He gave Emma a *what can I say?* shrug. "Sorry, how rude of me. I should have offered you a drink or something?"

"Emma."

"Emma. Sorry again." He went to a large cooler and pulled out a plastic water bottle and handed it to Emma.

Water! Ripples of wonderfully cold condensation ran down her fingers as she held the soft plastic bottle in her hand, then had to force her fingers to stop shaking as she unscrewed the lid.

Without taking a breath, she guzzled down the water greedily in one go. The thin plastic crinkled as she sucked every last drop out of the bottle, almost flattening its shape. The cool water felt wonderful, and for the moment, the dusty, twisted ball of razor wire that was clogging her throat vanished.

She sighed, then took a deep breath before handing the bottle back to the man. "Thanks."

"No problem." He stared at the misshapen piece of plastic in his hands.

Emma wiped her mouth with the back of her hand and noticed she had spilled some of the water down the front of her crop top, making the thin material cling to one of her breasts, her nipple protruding like a Whoppers candy ball. She could sense the man's eyes staring.

Conscious of his gaze, she folded her arms across her breasts.

The man gave a forced cough, his face turning beet red. "Uh...and you're alone, aren't you?"

"Yes," Emma replied, glancing at the child, who had gone back to hugging her father's leg. She seemed oblivious to the uncomfortable, silent exchange that had just transpired. *Don't worry, honey. You've got another ten years before you know the secret that it's his dick that makes a man tick.*

"I just thought I'd go for a hike by myself," Emma explained to the father. It sounded ridiculous but not completely implausible to her. Plenty of people, she imagined, went hiking into the woods on their own and got lost.

"Really?" The man eyed her suspiciously.

Emma regarded his pristine-looking clothing. Sturdy hiking boots with multicolored laces. Cargo pants with multiple pockets, and a formfitting long-sleeve shirt with a logo on the chest that looked like a skeletonized horse. And here she was in a pair of battered Converse sneakers, cutoff denim shorts, and a skimpy top. She wasn't exactly dressed for hiking. Hopefully, he would believe her.

She glanced back into the woods behind her again.

"It's just you, alone, isn't it?" he said as she turned back to him. This was the third time he had asked her the same question. His eyes were beginning to tear holes in her story.

"Yes," Emma almost snapped at him, instantly regretting her sudden shift in tone. "Look, I'm sorry." She rubbed her forehead, waves of frustration coming over her. "It's been a long day. I really need to make a phone call, contact my parents. They're probably out looking for me."

"I wish I could help," the man replied, smiling down at his daughter.

A thought hit Emma. "How did you get here? Did you park close by?" she asked, trying not to sound too desperate. But she was desperate. She needed to contact the police, while at the same time, didn't want to scare the little girl and her father.

The man shook his head. "We came into the park from the northern end. It's pretty deserted. It was about a half a day's hike."

Emma's hopes crashed. *Half a day's hike? My God. I thought it was just a small patch of woods, not Yellowstone!* She couldn't conceive that the man would agree to packing up their camp right now, and hike back with his daughter in the dark to where he had parked his car, just to help Emma. He would insist on waiting until the morning. By then it would be too late.

A small, sharp ball of pain began growing between her eyes, and she thought she was having an aneurysm. They would find her. Would find all three of them in that time. She had to tell them the truth, that at least two murderous psychos were pursuing her.

Emma glanced at the little girl. She would panic, scream, become difficult, possibly give away their location. Something about the father-daughter situation still niggled at Emma. Her mind kept returning to the bizarre notion of the father not having a cell phone on him. It made no sense.

Looking again at the man, she got the distinct feeling that she wasn't the only one who was lying. "Look, mister— "

"Jack. It's Jack."

The small ball of pain between Emma's eyes grew into a baseball. "Look—Jack! It's urgent. I really need to make a phone call."

"Daddy doesn't have a phone," the little girl scolded Emma. "He just said that." She looked up at her father lovingly for confirmation. "You don't have a cell phone, do you, Daddy? You left it at home. That's what we agreed on."

The man looked down at her, his eyes riddled with guilt. Then he let out a defeated sigh, and his face collapsed. "Just wait here a second," he said to Emma.

Bewildered, the little girl watched as her father, shoulders slumped and with his head down, walked to the small tent. He went inside, emerging a few moments later, carrying something in his hand.

Emma's heart began double-pumping when she saw what he was carrying.

His face glowed in the cell phone's glare as he thumbed the screen, entered his passcode, then handed the phone to Emma.

"Daddy! You promised!" The girl's expression crumpled into one of immense grumpiness.

He turned to his daughter and crouched down, so he was at her height. "I'm sorry, sweet pea. It's just for emergencies, that's all. I haven't been doing any work on it. I promise. I wasn't going to tell you, but Mommy insisted I bring it."

The girl folded her arms defiantly before looking away, her lips bowed in a tiny pout. "You promised!" she huffed, glaring at Emma as though it was somehow her fault her father had lied to her.

The man threw Emma a conciliatory shrug. "Sorry. But what can I say? I had good intentions."

Emma nodded and turned her attention back to the cell phone. Her eyes automatically flicked across the three-number sequence: nine-one-one. Her thumb hovered over the bright glass screen, salvation only three thumb presses away.

She paused and looked up.

What was that?

It sounded like a distant, guttural growling. Some kind of animal, mountain lion maybe? Surely not? The growling was getting louder, deeper, closing in on the three of them fast, too fast.

"What the hell is that?" the man asked, stepping up beside Emma.

She whirled around the small clearing, trying to pinpoint the exact location of the sound. One moment the sound seemed to be where she had come from. The next second, it sounded like it was circling them, getting louder, spiraling in toward them.

Two bright white eyes appeared out of the darkness to their right, not orbs but slitted and feline like a cat's. The growling intensified, growing more thunderous, deeper in tone and bass. Something large and angry was hurtling toward them, ripping through the undergrowth, churning up the dirt, tearing through bushes and smattering aside branches like brittle twigs, flattening everything in its locomotive wake.

Suddenly, the clearing was bathed in blinding light, as a huge, wide, bull-nosed grille smashed through the undergrowth. It wasn't a roaring animal. It was much worse: a six-liter, supercharged Hemi V8 engine—seven hundred galloping horses of raw power—lashed under the hood of a three-thousand-kilogram chariot made from cast iron, aluminum alloy, tempered glass, powder-coated hardened plastic, steel, rubber, and finished in glossy diamond black, that had rolled off the assembly plant in Sterling Heights, Michigan.

The massive RAM pickup truck shot into the clearing at nearly sixty miles per hour, heading straight for where Emma was standing.

37

DARK ANGEL

I stop running. There's no point. The sound of the truck has vanished. Turning, I look in every direction, the woods dark and once again silent around me.

My phone vibrates in my pocket, no ringtone. There is only one person who knows this number who can possibly be calling. It is her phone after all.

"Beatriz," I say, answering the call. "Sorry, I should have given you an update earlier."

"What's happening? I read your text a few hours ago. Did you find the log cabin?"

I hesitate. I don't want to lie to her, but should I tell her everything that's happened since I left the diner? We are a team, and I wouldn't have found Emma without her. So, I tell her everything, leaving out the part about the waitress, Frances Pridmore driving up here and having her neck broken by Pritchard. There's no need to tell Vega this. She may convince me to call in the authorities otherwise. I don't want to implicate her in my decision not to call the police. It's all on me. No one else. While I'm not comfortable with the decision, I've made up my mind. Finding Emma, who is still alive is all that matters to me. The dead remain dead. Nothing can bring them back.

"So, you are going after Emma?" she asks. "That would explain why you are in the forest."

I stare at the phone in my hand. Of course. It's her phone, which I imagine serves also as a tracking device. Vega knows exactly where I am, and where I've been. In a strange way it's comforting to know I'm not alone in this, even though I am.

"I agree with what you said about not contacting the police," Vega adds. "The police are hopeless," she scoffs in her heavy Peruvian accent. "Pritchard and this woman you've mentioned will escape for certain."

Vega knows what happened in the past when I tried apprehending Pritchard. "What can you tell me about where I am?" I ask, knowing that she probably has me up as a flashing blip on her computer screen. "Where exactly am I?" Perhaps there is something nearby, a road, landmark, ranger's hut that Emma will head toward. She'll try and find others. Campers, hikers, anyone who can help her. Hopefully, they won't be drawn into Pritchard's violence as Frances was.

"I can pinpoint your location to within a few meters, but apart from that I can't see anything else around you. I don't have that level of detail on my screen. You have been moving northeast and are in a large state forest. Pritchard could be anywhere, and so could Emma. I've been monitoring police communications for the last few hours in your area, and there has been nothing of significance. A DUI five miles away and a domestic dispute in Camilla. Apart from that, no one has reported anything about a pickup truck driving erratically and certainly nothing in the state forest you're in."

I guess it's now just down to my instincts to see if I can find Emma.

"However, there is something else that you might find useful," Vega adds. "About Emma. It might not be directly related to you finding her now, or Pritchard."

"What is it, Beatriz?" I ask. Right now, I need all the help I can get. Anything that can give me some insight into the young woman.

How she thinks, where she would go. I might be able to work out what she is likely to do next.

"I've been doing some background checking, and I found something interesting that happened to her while she was in high school. Apparently, there was an incident. I accessed her school database, logged into the student records, and found some interesting notes on her file."

By *accessed*, Vega means *hacked*. I give a grim smile.

"It mentions an incident where Emma attacked another girl in her class, broke her nose."

My heart sinks. Vega was right before. It's not exactly relevant now in helping me find Emma. "Anything else?" I ask.

"Well, the girl whose nose she broke didn't press charges, and from the notes I've read in the file, it seems like it all escalated from an argument over a young man."

That figures. Teenagers squabbling over the same guy.

Vega continues. "Emma was suspended for a few weeks, but then a few months later both the girl and the guy in question disappeared."

A prickle of interest suddenly hooks its claws into me. "What do you mean disappeared?"

"They simply vanished. As of now, they are both still registered as missing persons with the police department."

"How long ago was this, when they vanished?"

"About a year ago. Just after high school graduation. The police interviewed all the students in the class. I've already read through the student interview statements. I also accessed the local police database and read the interview statements. Emma was also brought in for questioning about the disappearance of the two. But she was eliminated as a person of interest. I got the distinct impression from reading the student interview statements, that most of her classmates believed that Emma and this other girl, who were best friends, had fallen out over this same guy."

My suspicions are confirmed. "So, they were best friends?"

"Correct."

I sit down and put my back against a tree and hold the phone close to my ear. "What's your take on it, Beatriz?"

"It does seem odd. My gut feeling tells me that Emma was somehow involved in the disappearance of the two. Jealousy perhaps. Retribution maybe for something."

"It would have to be for something pretty serious," I say. "If you're suggesting Emma was somehow involved in their disappearance. She did break the girl's nose. Anyone would think that would be enough retribution for stealing another girl's boyfriend, if that's what it was."

"Unless there was more to it," Vega continues. "Much more."

I think about it for a few moments. Would Emma do something to harm a fellow student at her school beyond a locker room–style physical attack? Her mother did say she was a fighter, and from what little I know of her, she seems like the type who would not back down in a fight. Especially if she was cornered.

"Thanks, Beatriz. Keep digging."

"I'll keep monitoring the local police chatter and send you silent messages only if I discover anything important. Be careful, Carolyn. Are you armed?"

"Yes," I lie.

I end the call and then tap the phone against my forehead, thinking. Maybe Emma is some kind of dark angel who does bring retribution on those who have harmed or who have wronged her. But how does that character assessment help me finding her right now?

Then a thought occurs to me. I know that she ran from the fallout shelter with her hands tied. It's only logical to assume her feet were also bound and that she somehow freed them but not her hands. She is resourceful and determined. So were many of Pritchard's previous victims. I can imagine all of them, with what little time they had, tried their best to escape too.

Yet, there is one thought that does concern me about Emma, especially after what Vega has just told me. Maybe Emma isn't going to keep running. Maybe she's going to stop and—I know it sounds crazy —she's going to try to seek some form of retribution against Pritchard and the woman by somehow turning the tables on them.

And that thought worries me the most. I set off again, heading in the direction where I thought I last heard the sound of a vehicle.

38

CARNAGE

They say that when you experience something so fast, so unexpected, and so gut-wrenchingly violent, time slows down.

That you can see in minute detail, every splinter of bone, every ribbon of torn flesh, every velvety-red droplet of blood spatter as it arcs in beautiful waves through the air before hitting your face. For Emma, however, time did not slow down. It did not elongate. And it certainly did not stop. It did the complete opposite: it compressed. Five seconds of brutal carnage shrank into less time than it took for two hearts to beat their next and final beat.

What saved Emma's life was her training, her ability to sense danger and then instinctively move her body out of harm's way before her brain had a chance to even process what was about to happen.

In the years to come, the horrendous moment, captured so quickly and so vividly inside her memory, would be replayed in a never-ending loop at an excruciatingly slow speed for the rest of her life. No matter how hard she tried, she would never erase the horrors of those brutal few seconds.

The massive front grille of the pickup, like a bull's charging head, had careened headlong into Jack and his daughter, shutting them from Emma's sight in a blur of exploding blood and bone. What remained of their bodies was ground into the dirt under the meaty all-terrain tires as the pickup plowed through the small clearing, crushing everything in its path. The log fire. The camp table. The camp chairs. The pink Barbie tea set. The ice cooler. And lastly, the two-person tent that was pitched at the opposite end under a small tree. With performance shocks, heightened ground clearance, and a massive front bull bar, the pickup was the ultimate off-road carnage wrecking ball.

It skidded sideways to a halt, leaving a torn path of destruction in its wake as though a meteor had crash-landed.

Emma found herself on her back, her face coated with blood. Dazed and uncertain, she struggled to an upright position and stared at the idling pickup. One side was smeared with brown-red gore, and a fragment of bone wrapped in strawberry-blonde hair was caught near the front fender.

The driver's side door slowly opened, and a man stepped down. He turned and surveyed the destruction, then gave a slow, almost proud nod of approval. "The guy at the dealership was right," Pritchard declared. "She sure is a beast."

Emma looked up at Pritchard. Their eyes met.

He gave her a satisfied smile. "Hey, little lady. How in God's name did I miss you?"

Emma blinked hard. *No! No! No! This can't be happening.* Somehow, Pritchard had driven through the woods to get here. They hadn't been on foot as she had imagined. It didn't matter how fast and how fit Emma was. She wasn't as fast as the massive pickup truck that they had used to reach her.

Looking around, she felt no immediate sorrow for the father and daughter. Not because she didn't have any emotions, but because she was overcome completely by the shock of it all. The time for mourning over the deaths would come much later. In the present moment, she was too wrapped up in bone-numbing shock to think of anything else. It had happened so fast, so violently, that the cogs in her brain had seized, could not generate any thought, emotion, or action.

Pritchard didn't move. He just stood, smiling at Emma.

Slowly, the cogs inside Emma's brain clicked one notch over, then stopped.

He had found her. There was no escape.

The cogs clicked over another notch, then stopped.

The passenger door of the pickup truck opened, and Dolly climbed down.

Another click, faster this time, the cogs struggling to gain momentum.

No matter where she went, how fast she ran, he would hunt her down.

Three clicks in a row this time, then the cogs stopped.

Dolly licked her lips as she stared at Emma. "You missed one." She gave a manic, hyena-like laugh. "Run over the bitch. And this time, don't miss."

The little singsong melody drifted back into Emma's consciousness.

Run, Emma. Run, Emma. Run, run, run.

Emma shook her head, like a dog shedding water from its coat. Her paralysis cleared as the cogs of her brain began turning and turning, not stopping.

Run, Emma. Run, Emma. Run, run, run. The melody grew steadily louder.

But where? Which way? How could she outrun the devil when he was riding his big black beast of death?

Somehow, Emma found the strength, the motivation to get to her feet.

Then, like a petrified rabbit, she bounded off into the tree line and vanished into the darkness.

39

ANOTHER

When taking another step could mean that her heart might explode in her chest, Emma finally stopped running.

Battered and bruised, her shins and knees crosshatched with cuts and abrasions, she collapsed on the ground, then crawled on her hands and knees to the nearest tree. With her back resting against the tree trunk, she closed her eyes. Sickening images immediately flooded behind her eyelids.

She blinked open. It was a mistake to shut them. She didn't want to see the bloodshed, even though it was still fresh and raw. *Why? Why did they have to die? Why does anyone need to die like that?*

As much as she tried, Emma couldn't rid her mind of the brutality she had just witnessed. Her stomach twisted. She turned, rolled back onto all fours, and puked up what little water she had just consumed that the father had given her. With eyes wide open, she waited, panting like a dog for the waves of sickness to pass. Once they subsided, she wiped her mouth with the back of her hand and sat back down against the tree, staring off vacantly into the collage of charcoal grays and muted blacks. Slowly, she began hitting the back of her head against the rough tree bark, like she was trying to knock some sense into her head when nothing made sense anymore.

What had they, the father and daughter, done to deserve this? It was all her fault. She had brought death and mayhem to two innocent people. Was it some kind of sick penance for stealing—borrowing her mom's car? All she wanted to do was see her father, the man whose DNA she shared. Was that such a crime?

Emma wasn't a religious person. Neither was her mom. And she wasn't exactly going to pray now either. She looked up through the spidery limbs of the branches above to the cold, dark sky beyond. "Fuck you," she murmured. A twist of nausea gripped her, and she turned and puked again.

Maybe he was listening.

Emma rested her head against the tree trunk again. Her bones felt cold, her limbs ached, her mouth a canyon of sand. Closing her eyes again, she saw bloody strawberry-blonde hair twisted around a fragment of crushed skull wedged near the front fender of the pickup truck. Her stomach convulsed, but there was nothing left inside to purge.

She didn't know how long she had dozed for, but she woke with a start. Her eyes scanned the dark, brooding shapes around her. Somewhere in the murkiness, something scuttled, rustling through the undergrowth. She felt better now, and slowly she began trying to comprehend how they had found her, how they had driven the pickup truck through the woods at that speed.

Then it dawned on Emma. There must be tracks wide enough to drive a vehicle along. She certainly hadn't seen any. Then again, she wasn't really looking for them, either, as she was running for her life.

Perhaps they had seen the glow of the campfire and then saw Emma standing there with the father and daughter. The thought of the two again brought a fresh wave of queasiness over her. Taking a few deep breaths seemed to work.

No. She needed to focus on what to do, not on what had been done, no matter how horrendous and how gut-wrenching it had been. And yet, as she thought about it, it still made no sense. How did they find her so quickly?

In the bloody mayhem that ensued, she had dropped the cell phone the father had given her. Another mistake. For a moment, Emma contemplated going back, seeing if she could find it. Surely, they wouldn't expect her to return there.

She wondered where they were now. One thing was for certain, now that she knew they were in a pickup truck, she would stay well clear of any trails or any dirt roads if she discovered them. Then how was she going to find other people? Someone who could help her. The father had said that it was half a day's hike to where he had parked his car. Was that the start of a trailhead? He had also said it was deserted, meaning that the chances of Emma coming across other hikers were slim. It was obvious now that she had crossed into a state forest.

As Emma began weighing her limited options, it was becoming obvious that she had to go deeper into the woods, where the pickup surely could not reach. That tactic, however, would take her away from civilization, not closer. Away from finding any help at all. And she would probably end up getting lost. A cynical chuckle escaped her lips. She was lost now, so it didn't really matter. Maybe getting lost and dying of exposure or thirst was better than running into those two psychos again. At least she would die on her terms, not someone else's.

She glanced up at the moon again. Its pale skull-like face that bathed the woods in an eerie glow seemed to mock her.

Maybe she could find one of those placard maps she had seen in state forests before that would show her location and a way out of the place. Emma shook the thought from her mind, thinking she'd have more luck believing that Harry Styles would show up asking her to the Grammys as his date.

The thought of going back, picking her way through the bloodied remains of the campsite, searching for the cell phone, then accidentally touching a foot or a hand brought on another wave of nausea. Emma swallowed hard and waited until it passed.

Then there was the log cabin. She had only spent the briefest of seconds in there searching. There could be a phone there, something she could use. Like returning to the campsite, the thought of going back to the cabin was fraught with risk. It didn't sit easily with her, and she doubted if she could retrace her steps and find it again.

Waiting it out till daylight may not be such a bad idea after all. Then again, she would be more exposed. At least by using the cover of darkness, she could move easier. But to where? She started pulling at her hair in frustration.

Two people were dead, and the guilt of that fact lay heavily on her.

She needed to take action. It wasn't in her nature to just sit and wait for help to arrive. If she did, she had an uncanny feeling that the murderers would just find her again.

Getting to her feet, Emma looked around, almost expecting the pickup truck to come barreling out of the darkness and flatten her like how it had done to the father and daughter. It almost gave the two occupants a supernatural tinge to them like they were not human, which they weren't, in Emma's mind.

They were *inhuman*.

The hairs on the back of Emma's neck bristled. She looked around her, sensing something was not right. She pulled back into the shadows of the tree, her eyes scanning the woods around her.

A shape moved among the trees, maybe fifty yards away from her. It wasn't an animal. It was walking upright, not fast but not slow either. Emma waited and watched as the shape then melted into the darkness and was gone.

What was that? she wondered, her heart almost in her mouth. Was there someone else here? Maybe another person, one of the ones she had seen standing near the cabin when she paused in the doorway of the fallout shelter.

Slowly, Emma made off in the opposite direction.

40

HORRORS

I pause and squint into the darkness. I thought I heard something. A branch or twig snap maybe? Is it Emma, or could someone be camping out here?

Shadows ripple and slither over each other as I strain my eyes to where I heard something. Could be just an animal, like the one that had killed the deer. It's gone now. Maybe it's just my imagination, but I distinctly felt something, like someone was there, moving in the darkness.

I search the ground, not sure what I'm looking for. I could be going in circles for all I know. Maybe some disturbance, broken twig, broken branch, undergrowth flattened, anything that may give me some clue as to where Emma has gone. But everything looks disturbed in the darkness.

My cell phone feels like it's burning a hole in my pocket, calling for my attention. The niggling is still in the back of my mind to call the police, the FBI, get them involved. I'm torn. With every step I take, I feel like the trail is getting cold.

I strain again to listen.

Nothing. The sound is gone. It came from my left, or was it my right? Sound waves don't move in straight lines. They can bounce off trees, rocks, buildings, get filtered and buffeted, smothered and absorbed by the surroundings. Honestly, I have no clue where the sound came from. I was right before. It was my imagination. Me wanting to hear something, wanting Emma to call out for help.

Aaron Wood is on speed dial. The thought of calling him seems enticing. Calling him, sending up a flare, so to speak, would be an admission of failure. I can do this on my own, but am I risking Emma's life in the process just to satisfy my ego? No. I push aside any thoughts of that.

There's enough moonlight for me to continue, and I pick up the pace. The ground slopes down, and the vegetation abruptly stops as I step out onto a wide, flattened section. The damage is manmade. Crouching down, I activate the flashlight on my cell phone, then pan it slowly to the right and see equally spaced lines carving across the ground. Tire tracks. Excitement hits me.

A vehicle has been through here, and recently. Some blades of foliage are slowly moving, bending back to their original position. There's also a slight tinge in the air. Exhaust gas. Carbon monoxide. It's faint, but I can definitely smell it.

It has to be Pritchard and that bitch in their pickup truck.

Shit! Panic fills me, and I quickly fumble with my cell phone, turning off the flashlight. In the darkness I hold my breath, the sounds of the woods chattering around me. An owl gives a mournful hoot somewhere in the distance. Christ, they could've seen me. I might as well have just sent up a flare to give away my location.

Listening intently, I look around. The only sound, though, is my heavy breathing. It was a stupid rookie mistake. My eyes adjust again, and I pick up on the tire tracks curving away slightly to the left. It must be some sort of old track, not a public dirt road where the foliage has been properly cut back. The trees have been clearly cut down, leaving bare stumps, clearing a path wide enough for vehicles to pass unhindered, giving it the appearance of a hidden road used by forest workers or park rangers.

As I follow the trail through the foliage, it winds back and forth around larger, more established trees. The ground is still rough, but the dirt and rocks are beaten smooth. Definitely, heavy trucks have been through here on a regular basis.

Cresting a small verge, a smell hits me. A bitter smokiness in the air. Woodsmoke. It's coming from up ahead, I'm certain.

Then I notice a nearby tree on the edge of the trail. One of the low branches has been ripped away, not cleanly cut by a saw, but snapped off, leaving a shredded joint on the trunk and a trampled branch on the ground. Slightly farther, but on the opposite side, I find another fallen branch. Once again, it's been ripped, not cut from the trunk. The devastation gets more noticeable the farther I walk. The ground becomes increasingly rippled, deep furrows in the dirt. I can just make out wide tracks, likely made from off-road tires, something with a lot of grip. The ground is churned. I turn back and look into the darkness from where I have come, then look back at the tire tracks. A vehicle came through here at speed, accelerating when it reached this point, swaying side to side almost uncontrollably, ripping away branches from the trees on the sides as it flew by. I picture Pritchard hunkered down behind the wheel of his truck, eyes blazing, face twisted in a manic grin as he's flooring the gas pedal, desperate to find Emma, or me. Not me, though. While he will try to kill me when we meet again, it's Emma who he really wants. She's the one who has escaped. In a way, I have been his prisoner, too, but my only escape is of a different kind.

The pale moonlight reveals something ahead, a clearing between the trees. I move forward again, my eyes and ears attuned to the slightest sound. I reach a small clearing and see something glowing in the middle. The embers of a dying fire, smoldering logs that have been scattered, smoke rising from them. As I take in the scene, my gut tightens. Twisted camp chairs, a table that's been obliterated. Dark, glistening smudges in the dirt like spilled red wine, but it's not wine. An orange tarp ripped and tattered on the ground. Then I realize it's not a tarp, but the remains of a small tent, wide tire marks tattooed across its surface, the seams threaded with broken tent poles.

I swallow hard as I catch sight of something. I'm not sure what it is. It looks like a small scarecrow, twisted horribly, like it has been pulled inside out. Sharp-nailed fingers drum over my scalp when I realize what I'm looking at. It's part of a torso, a man's, I think. I can't be certain. There's no head, only an arm, and part of a leg attached. It's like he swallowed a grenade.

I look away, then catch sight of a small, pink object to my left. I pick it up. It's a tiny toy pink teapot. *No!* Pure misery engulfs me and my heart splits. *No! Not a child. Please let it not be a child.*

Then I find her—or what's left of her—near the flattened tent. A bloodied tumbleweed of small limbs wrapped in a blood-soaked pink dress with a heart-shaped pattern. Half her skull is missing, ripped away. My own heart turns to brittle ice, and my fingers claw into my chest.

Breathe, Carolyn, breathe.

Tears try to force their way into my eyes, but I grit my teeth and push them back. I need to assess the scene, walk it again, take everything in. See who else is dead. So far, there's one adult male and a small child, a female as far as I can tell. There may be more.

Suppressing my anger, I walk the clearing, trying to piece together what has happened here, a nightmare I need to decipher. It looks like a campground that's been run over by a tank. After several passes, I've seen enough. Emma is not here. There are only two bodies: father and daughter, I gather.

Pritchard did this. There can be no other explanation.

Was Emma here, too? Had she stumbled across the pair and had asked for help?

A likely scenario that's growing in my head is that Emma came across them, tried to get help, telling them what had happened, that she was being chased by two murderous monsters. Pritchard caught up to her in his pickup, tried to run her over, and in the process, killed two innocent people.

I survey the carnage one more time, trying to work out if there's definitely not a third body here. I feel selfish, callous, like a cold-hearted bitch with how I'm thinking. A small glimmer of hope touches me when I'm done. Two dead, no Emma. There's nothing I can do for the dead; I'll deal with that later. For now, it looks like whatever happened here, Emma somehow survived. Like the jackrabbit I had seen when she ran from the fallout shelter, she's probably taken off again and running blindly through the woods.

Time is not on my side, though, and Pritchard seems determined to kill any and everyone who gets in his way. I've got to figure out which way his pickup truck left the clearing, then hopefully, it'll be a lot easier to track him if he's using the trail I just found. I have no choice now; I need to work out the exit point of the vehicle from this clearing. He's long gone from here, so I turn on the flashlight of my cell phone and begin searching the perimeter of the clearing. It's difficult. So much dirt has been plowed up.

After a few moments, I find the exit point on the opposite side. It's another rough trail, wide enough to accommodate a pickup truck. The trees on either side of the opening have had their branches trimmed back on one side, creating a hollow in the foliage. Crouching down, I pan the light across the ground to see a myriad of tire tracks, all different widths and depths, crisscrossing each other. There's nothing I can distinguish from the tread pattern I saw before. Maybe that was also the sound I heard earlier, his pickup leaving here.

I've found what I believe to be another hidden trail, and I'm going to follow it, unsure of where it's going to lead me or what horrors await along the way.

41

NOWHERE TO HIDE

The sight of the vehicle sitting across the open ground struck fear in Emma.

Its headlights lit up the woods like two searchlights. A dark shape was standing next to the front grille, and from where she crouched in the tree line, Emma could tell it wasn't the same truck that had torn through the campsite before.

Emma crept forward, unsure of what she was looking at.

Something buzzed and crackled, voices in the background mixed with static near the truck. Then she caught sight of the decal emblazoned on the side of the vehicle: U.S. Park Ranger.

Relief washed over her, and she stumbled forward.

It wasn't Pritchard and Dolly in the black pickup truck. It was a different vehicle, a two-door Jeep Wrangler.

A man standing at the hood turned as Emma emerged from the woods. He did a double take, as though he couldn't believe what he was seeing.

"Please, please, you have to help me," she cried, her arms outstretched.

The man ran to her and took her by the shoulders just before she was about to collapse. "Miss., what happened? Are you okay?"

The two-way radio clipped on his belt crackled with the static of voices.

She bowed her head, then mumbled, "Water. I need water."

The man eased her to the ground, before hurrying back to the Jeep, pulling something out of the center console. He rushed back, unscrewed the lid, and offered the water bottle.

Emma snatched it from his hand and drank. Water sloshed out of the sides of her mouth, and she tilted her head back and gulped. Throwing up all the water she had previously drunk had made her thirst insatiable. And she felt hot all of a sudden, like she had a temperature.

"Hey, take it easy," he said. "There's no rush."

Emma drained the bottle in a matter of seconds. Like osmosis, she could almost feel the water being drawn into her flesh, cold and replenishing her. Bringing her back to life. She glanced up at the man; he had a friendly face, young, and a name tag on his uniform: Lawson. She also noticed he was wearing a gun.

"You're police?"

The man shook his head. "I'm a law enforcement ranger, with the National Park Service. That's why I'm armed."

Emma breathed a sigh of relief. So he was a ranger. But at least he had a gun.

The man kneeled and watched her eagerly. "What happened? Did you get lost?"

Emma tried to form the words but couldn't get them out quick enough. "No. No. They... they...are chasing me."

She was exhausted, having run for what seemed like an eternity. Her body began to tremble and shake, the shock of everything suddenly becoming too much for her.

The man's eyes narrowed. "Chasing you? Who is chasing you?" Before she could answer, he returned to the Jeep and came back with a blanket and wrapped it around her shoulders.

"Just slow down. Take your time. Everything is okay."

Emma looked around. Everything was not okay. They were out there looking for her right now.

She shook her head, trying to assemble the jumble of emotions she was feeling into some logical order. "No. Not safe. I... They kidnapped me."

"Kidnapped? By who?"

"I...don't know. Two people. A man. A woman."

Emma tried to think back. Breaking down on the side of the road. Waking up chained to a bed. The dungeon, then escaping to the cabin. Being captured again. Then brought back to the dungeon. Then escaping again. Suddenly, dread sliced into her throat. She'd almost forgotten. Another memory she had locked away in another room down the dark passageway where others were hidden. The father. The daughter. Blood-soaked images came flooding back. A demon had been let loose again. The young girl's pulverized body. The tangled mess of blonde hair. The smashed tent. Blood and gore smeared down one side of the pickup.

Emma brought up a dribble of water as her stomach convulsed.

"Hey, take it easy," the man cautioned.

Take it easy? How can I take it easy? "No, you don't understand!" Emma shrieked, grabbing the man's shirt with her fingers, pulling at him. She glared into his eyes. "They killed two people! Murdered them, right in front of my eyes. I was there!" The words came tumbling out like the blabbering rant of a crazy loon.

The man's face hardened. "Who killed two people? Are they hurt? Are you sure they're dead?" He shook Emma forcefully by the shoulders. "Where are they?"

Emma clutched at her chest. It was like she couldn't get enough air into her lungs. Panic riled through her as a wave of sweaty heat ignited in her. *What's wrong with me?* She looked up at the man again, saw his face multiply, two, three, four overlaying faces staring back at her. She blinked hard and looked again. "I...don't know. All I know is that they killed them." Emma felt dizzy, her skin hot and clammy. *What's the matter with me?* The dizzy spell passed, and she looked at the man again. "Please, call the police. Tell them."

The mike of the two-way radio attached to the man's lapel squawked.

Emma looked at the radio. "But you know!" she shrieked. "That's why you're here."

Confusion flooded the man's eyes. "Ma'am, I don't know about anyone that has been killed. I'm just responding to a call that was made by some campers a few miles south of here. Just a disturbance. Apparently, some four-wheel drive has been tearing through the woods, causing a ruckus. That's all. I thought it was kids joyriding. But now you're saying someone's been killed?"

Emma nodded. "Two people. Run over. Murdered. Not an accident. Not kids."

The man shook his head in disbelief. "You've got to calm down, tell me where this was. The exact location. Do you think you can show me?"

Emma looked around. She had no sense of direction anymore, of where she was going or where she had been, let alone trying to work out how to get back to the campsite. And she didn't want to go back. Didn't want to see the carnage again.

"I don't know," she mumbled. "I can't remember. I don't know which direction it was." Her body ached, and her left ankle throbbed. She must have twisted it when she was running. She glanced at the man's hip to where a handgun sat nestled in its holster. It gave her some comfort. He was armed. He could stop them. Even kill them. She glanced up at him. "Look, you've got to get help. Call for backup or whatever. They're dangerous. Murderers, and now they want to murder me."

The man took out a notebook. "I need your name, any details you can give me, someone I can call."

Emma shook her head. "Don't worry about me. I'll be fine. You've got to get help." She reached out and grabbed his shirt again. "Please." Spittle flicked from her lips. "You don't under-stand. They will find me. They'll find us. They won't stop until they do."

The man gave her a skeptical look, almost as if he were now starting not to believe her. "Have you...taken anything, ma'am?"

Disbelief crowded Emma's mind. *Taken anything?*

Reaching out, he attempted to open one of Emma's eyelids wider to take a closer look.

Emma battered his hand away. "No, no! I'm telling the truth. You have to get help." She watched in disbelief as his eyes did a slow up and down of her body that made her feel dirty, tainted, like she were a criminal.

He cocked an eyebrow. "Ma'am, I'm going to need you to turn out your pockets."

"What?"

"Have you been taking any substances?"

"No, you don't understand," Emma pleaded. "Get help. Now!"

The man stood up, reached for his two-way and pressed the button. "This is Lawson. I've got a party camper here. She's taken something, and I found her wandering around. I'm going to bring her in."

Emma looked up at the man. *Party camper?* "But...but..." She got to her feet, feeling a little giddy. "I haven't taken any drugs—"

Suddenly, the darkness turned to daylight, and everything around them was bathed in a brilliant white light.

Emma turned in horror to see a black mass, like a charging rhinoceros, come hurtling out of the woods.

The ranger looked up and froze.

Elbowing the ranger aside, Emma ran toward where the Jeep was parked.

The glare of the headlights zeroed in on where the ranger was standing as he went for his gun.

As she ran, Emma heard the crack of gunshots. Once, twice, then a sickening thump. Something sailed past her head, like a giant bowling pin, before crashing to the earth a few feet from her right.

She kept on running.

The pickup swerved, fishtailed, before driving headlong into a thick tree with a thunderous crash of metal and glass.

Reaching the Jeep, Emma flopped to her belly and crawled under the chassis. Looking sideways along the ground, she craned her neck and could see the pickup. The front end was folded like the bellows of an accordion, into a large tree, liquid spilling on the ground beneath, wisps of steam hissing from under the crumpled hood.

Her eyes tracked across the ground to where the disfigured body of the ranger lay in a twisted mess. Emma could feel her heart thrum against the ground where her chest was pressed.

She looked back at the pickup. A door opened, and a heavy black work boot landed on the ground, tentatively at first, then another boot. The person stood there for a moment, the ankles and shins swaying slightly. "Christ damn!" they cursed. The boots staggered forward, then stopped again. "Fucker knew how to shoot."

Emma slid behind the axle some more, trying to hide her body. It was Pritchard, all right, even though all she could see were his boots. Those ugly, heavy work boots, with the scuffed and scarred toes and the slit with part of the steel cap beneath showing.

The boots turned and pointed directly to where she lay under the chassis of the Jeep and began walking toward her. Tentative steps at first, they had a Frankenstein stagger to them.

A crackle of static, then a voice came from somewhere, and Emma glanced to where the twisted body of the ranger lay. She watched as the boots suddenly changed direction and headed toward the body, then stopped. A hand came into view and reached down and unclipped the two-way radio, the fingers of the other hand touching the name badge on the shirt.

The mike clicked and Pritchard's calm voice sent a chill through Emma's body. "Lawson, here. Nothing to report."

A garbled voice that Emma couldn't make out came from the two-way.

Then another click of the mike. "I think it was just a hoax. The girl is gone. I'll take another look around and then head back shortly. But like I said. It's a hoax. It's all quiet."

The dispatcher confirmed and radioed off.

The boots didn't move, and Emma could see Pritchard prize something from the hand of the dead forest ranger. Then to her horror, the boots turned and resumed their trek toward where she was hiding under the Jeep. Ten feet from her and she heard a gun being racked: a round being pushed into the chamber.

He was coming to kill her.

And there was nowhere to hide.

42

NO SENSE

Thick yellow coils jacked up each suspension strut of the Jeep, affording Emma enough head clearance under the chassis to push up on her forearms and worm her body back, away from the side where Pritchard was approaching from.

She could feel her legs poking out in the open on the other side, and if need be, she would push herself out completely and make a run for it, putting the Jeep between her and Pritchard. Yet she was unsure if he had seen her scoot beneath the Jeep. Maybe he was just seeing what he could salvage from the Jeep. He already had taken the ranger's handgun.

Movement caught the edge of her eye, and Emma glanced toward where the pickup had crashed. Another set of feet, Dolly's, she guessed, had emerged from the passenger side. They teetered for a moment.

"Where'd the bitch go?" came Dolly's unmistakable growl.

"You okay?"

"Damn airbag broke my nose, I think."

"That's it? You didn't get hit?"

"No, I'm fine. Bastard was a lousy shot. Where did she go?"

"No idea," Pritchard called back. Pritchard's boots didn't move.

He was that close. Emma could see the individual scuff marks on the toes of his heavy work boots—and something else. Blood? There was blood on the toe of one of his boots. His blood, she hoped. The crash must have injured him. He was bleeding.

"Well, she must be here somewhere," Dolly whined. "We both saw her. Look for her."

Emma's stomach tightened.

Dolly began lumbering over toward where Pritchard was standing, pausing only momentarily over the twisted body of the ranger. "Stupid bastard," she cursed before kicking the twisted mass with her foot.

Moments later, they stood side by side, two sets of feet just ten feet away, pointing directly at Emma.

"Maybe she took off again," Pritchard suggested.

"Maybe."

To Emma, Pritchard's words sounded dull, empty, but they gave her a glimmer of hope. He hadn't seen her crawl under the Jeep. If he had, then he wouldn't be standing ten feet away from where she was trying her hardest not to piss in her shorts with fear.

Dolly's feet turned away. "Come on, we're wasting time, then. Let's go."

"Go, how?" Pritchard shot back.

Then Emma heard a jingling.

"What's that?" Dolly asked.

"Keys. I pulled them off the ranger. The truck is a write-off. It won't be going nowhere. We'll take the Jeep."

"Good idea," Dolly replied. "But let's get going. I don't want her to get too far."

Emma's bladder was at bursting point, the sudden urge to pee almost unbearable.

Then both Dolly and Pritchard climbed into the Jeep above her. She could hear the ignition click over inches from her head before the engine roared to life.

Panicked, she quickly pulled her legs in and twisted her hips, lining up her body between the front and back wheels under the chassis so they wouldn't crush her when they drove off.

The Jeep kicked into gear and rolled forward inch by inch in a straight line. Keeping her arms pressed against her sides—and her thighs, knees, and feet firmly together—Emma lay ramrod straight, her face pressed into the dirt, as the Jeep passed over her and she was out in the open again. She knew if either of them were to look in the side mirrors, they would probably see her lying on the ground behind them, as though disgorged from the back of the Jeep.

The Jeep kept rolling forward, until eventually it disappeared into the woods, Emma only tilting her head at the very last moment to see the taillights fading into the darkness.

Spluttering out a mouthful of dirt and breathing an enormous sigh of relief, Emma rolled onto her back and looked up at the moonlit sky. How had she escaped? Was luck finally on her side? It never had been in the past. She had never been this close to death before, and now, through the barest of margins had managed to escape it again.

But for how much longer? She glanced at the tattoo on her forearm. *Memento mori. Remember, you must die.*

"Not today," she said grimly before getting to her feet and dusting herself off. Then she whipped down her shorts and emptied her bladder.

After she was done peeing, Emma searched the crumpled pickup truck. Steam was still hissing from under the massive hood that was bent into a V-shape, and a huge puddle had pooled under the front tires. The truck was going nowhere.

Emma searched inside, seeing if she could salvage anything. But there was nothing. It had been stripped clean. No personal effects. Loose change. Nothing. The car was spotless inside. Not even a fast-food wrapper. Then she realized why. It was so Pritchard could make a quick escape, if he, for whatever reason, was involved in a motor vehicle accident. There would be no ID, nothing to trace back to him, not even a single receipt for gas. The man was meticulous, relentless. There was not even registration, proof of ownership in the glove box.

The two-way radio! With all the panic and anxiety, she had just experienced, Emma had forgotten about it. Pritchard had used the two-way radio to tell the dispatcher that everything was fine. He pretended to be the ranger, and the dispatcher had fallen for it. Now she could use it to call someone and tell them what happened.

She rushed to where the twisted corpse of the ranger lay. This time, she believed it wasn't her fault. She hadn't murdered him. Pritchard had. It was the same as with the father and daughter. Yet she felt more guilt with them than she did looking down now at the body at her feet. She was becoming immune to seeing death. She had seen so much of it in the last few hours.

She shook her head. *What? Where's the radio?*

It was gone.

She glanced back to where the Jeep had driven off. Pritchard must have taken it.

Damn! She clenched her fists, wanting to scream.

43

SNEAKY BASTARD

Emma stood in the crooked beams of the headlights of Pritchard's pickup truck, contemplating why he had again found her so easily and so quickly.

At the campsite, she had been there, what, five minutes? Ten at the most before he roared through. Until then, she hadn't heard or seen the pickup truck at all in the woods. It was like it just appeared out of thin air. The same was with the ranger. Again, no forewarning.

She had no cell phone. He had taken that from her when he kidnapped her. People could be tracked by their cell phone signal, even if it was turned off. So, it must be something else. He seemed to know where she was or where she was going.

She had on what she wore from the very start of this nightmare. A crop top, cutoff jean shorts, and an old pair of Converse sneakers and socks. All these were now tattered, covered in grime, sweat, and blood.

So how did he know where she was?

Her fingers probed the two front pockets of her shorts. It was pointless, though. There was nothing there. Except for the Swiss Army knife Pritchard had left behind for her to find.

The knife?

Emma's mind caved in at the sheer stupidity of what she was thinking. *Could it be?*

She slipped it out, held it up in the beam of the headlights. It was just a simple Swiss Army knife you could get from any hardware store or online. Turning it over in her hands, she examined it more closely. It was about four inches long, maybe half an inch thick. On one side, a small corkscrew sat recessed into the plastic case. She slid the fingernail of her thumb into the groove on the side of the main blade and unfolded it. The blade, like the case, was covered in crusty dried blood. Her blood.

There was a small pair of scissors that she pulled out next. They had a curve of thin metal to act as a spring between each scissor blade. Next, she unfolded the can-opener tool, which had a snub-nosed end so it could be used as a flathead screwdriver. Then another smaller blade and finally a bottle opener with a wider snub nose. That was it. There were no other tools, and with them all pulled out, the penknife resembled a red-bodied spider with mismatching metal legs.

Then she spotted a raised ridge on the other side of the case next to the corkscrew. It took some effort to fit her fingernail in the small groove to pull it open. It seemed to be like another blade, almost hidden. But it was there. It took her a few attempts until finally a small, narrow, scalpel-like spike swung open and locked into place perpendicular to the body of the case.

She smiled, then folded away every other tool back into its rightful place, just leaving the small spike open. Gripping the case but allowing the spike to pass between the gap between her index and forefinger, she closed her fingers, making a fist.

Her smile grew wider.

Now it was like she was holding a set of brass knuckles with a steel spike poking out between her fingers. Knives weren't really her thing, didn't know how to use them properly in a fight, nor did she want to. She knew how to defend against them, but now, admiring her clenched fist with a half inch of sharpened spike poking between her fingers, this was more her style. She threw a few practice punches, quick, snappy jabs, visualizing herself burying the spike seven or eight times into Pritchard's face or Dolly's throat. *Bam! Bam Bam!*

Releasing her fingers, she carefully began pushing the scalpel blade back into its channel, then stopped. She tilted the case into the light some more, then saw it. A sliver of plastic, as flat as a SIM card but half the size, as though it had been cut lengthwise. Emma tried shaking the object loose, but it wouldn't budge. Searching the ground, she found a small shard of orange plastic, part of the truck's side light that had shattered. Carefully she worked the thin shard of plastic into the slot, then slowly moved it back and forth until the object came loose, and she tipped it into her palm.

My God.

It was tiny, with a small circuit pattern on it. It was electronic, she could tell, a microchip of some sort. "Sneaky bastard," she muttered, looking at the object.

Now it all made sense. It was all part of the sneaky game, except Pritchard, the instigator, was cheating, stacking the deck so he couldn't lose. Leaving Emma the penknife was as deliberate as it was stupid for her thinking it was just a careless mistake by him.

Let the fun and games begin. Isn't that what he had said to her?

Sure, he had used chloroform to knock her out and carry her back to her prison cell again after she had escaped the first time. However, Emma felt none of the severe side effects from the first time when he had used the chemical to snatch her from the side of the road. Nausea, dizziness, headaches. She hadn't felt any of that the second time when he had used it on her. Why? Because he had given her a lighter dose, knocking her unconscious for maybe ten minutes at the most. He had bound both her wrists and ankles because he wanted her to work, not make it too easy. But he left the penknife, too, as insurance, giving her an innocent tool that also hid a tracking device.

He was a hunter, and he wanted to hunt her. Not to simply

slaughter a hapless animal. He wanted Emma to escape and make it a competition. A game. Her against him.

Would he have told Dolly? How would he explain that to her, that it was just a game? Was she in on it, too? Emma didn't think so. Her escaping meant that Dolly was deprived of the perverted pleasures she had craved so much.

No, Dolly wasn't in on the game. It was Pritchard's dirty secret, and Dolly was clueless about it. Dolly would never have her way with Emma. Pritchard made sure of it. They had argued after they discovered Emma in the cabin, searching for the truck keys. He had other plans for Emma.

She thought for a moment. Then it struck her. *Of course.* Subliminally, Pritchard was controlling the show behind Dolly's back. While he appeared to be taking orders from her, it was he who was controlling everything. Manipulating both Dolly and Emma, too.

Emma looked at the small device in her palm. So *what do I do now?*

Stepping away out of the light of the headlights and into the shadows, she drew a hand back, a tight fist around the tracking chip, then stopped.

Emma pursed her lips, her mind thinking. Slowly, she lowered her arm and unfolded her fingers. The chip was still there in the middle of her palm. No. She wasn't going to be manipulated. She thought of the dead. The father and daughter ruthlessly mowed down. Now the ranger. Three people were dead without a second thought. Pritchard had deliberately missed Emma on both occasions in his truck. Again, it seemed too easy for him, and he knew it.

Emma glanced over to the spot where the Jeep had been parked. He knew she was hiding under the chassis. But it would be like shooting fish in a barrel if he had got down and shot her there and then. He followed Dolly's lead, driving off, acting as though Emma had taken off into the woods again. How long could he keep up the charade with Dolly? He wanted to hunt—on his own. That much was obvious. Maybe Dolly was becoming a burden? For Pritchard, there was room for only one player in the game. Him.

Emma glanced again at the chip in her hand and smiled.

Taking out the penknife she carefully placed the chip back into the narrow channel where she had found it, before closing the spike over it, then slipping it back safely in her pocket.

Two can play at this game.

44

ROAD TO HELL

Jesus!

I veer off the dirt track and throw myself into the undergrowth.

I almost didn't see it, two red lights in the distance. The taillights of a vehicle. The taillights aren't moving. The vehicle looks like it's stopped.

I edge forward through the undergrowth, approaching the driver's side. The headlights are on, the dirt track ahead lit up like daylight. It's not a pickup truck, not the RAM truck I was expecting. It's a smaller SUV, a Jeep Wrangler, I think.

Creeping closer, a decal on the door becomes visible: U.S. Park Ranger. My heart sinks; it's not Pritchard. All might not be lost, however. Maybe they can help me.

Still using the cover of the woods, I edge closer. Inside the dark cabin, a light suddenly flares from a cell phone. I can see it, in the ranger's hand, but not their face. They're calling someone.

Three more feet and I'm square against the side door, watching them from the woods.

The driver is thumbing their cell phone, their face lit by the glow of the screen... It's Pritchard!

Oh shit.

It's Pritchard. I blink hard. I must be hallucinating. It can't be him.

I look again. It's definitely him.

What the hell is he doing in a park ranger SUV?

I duck back into the shadows. It makes little sense. He's just parked there, looking at his cell phone. I angle around some more, and then I partially see a woman in the passenger's seat. A woman? I can't see her clearly, but it's definitely not Emma. I catch a glimpse of gray hair, the loose jowls of her chin. I can't see her face completely, but I know it's the woman from the cabin. His partner in murder.

It doesn't matter now what happened to his pickup. He obviously crashed it driving like a maniac through the woods. I imagine it got fairly battered too when he mowed down those two innocent people back at the campsite. Now he's commandeered another vehicle and probably killed the ranger as well. Another victim to add to his murderous body count.

I have to stop him.

Peering through the bushes, I see he's still checking his phone. It's like he's searching for something, not sure of which direction to go. Maybe he's called up a park map. There's no point in me doing the same thing on my cell phone. I've got no idea where I'm going—but I do now. I'm going where they are going. They're searching for Emma and will lead me to her. It's the only viable strategy I have.

As I watch, he lowers his cell phone, then mumbles something to the woman. The Jeep slowly drives off, the soft crunch of gravel under the tires.

If he maintains that low speed, I'll be able to keep up on foot, hang back in the darkness and follow them.

I wait until the Jeep is about twenty yards away before I ease out of the woods and slip in behind it, walking on the dirt track. He is still driving slowly, cautiously. He's searching for someone or a location.

The track is fairly flat, and as I follow, tucked in behind the Jeep, I wonder where they are going. After a hundred yards, the track starts to slope upward before curving to the left. The Jeep slows to a crawl, and I stop. Then it makes a right turn, the headlights bobbing over the undulating ground.

I follow again, praying that he doesn't suddenly hit the gas. The track narrows, more rocks and deeper grooves, the woods pressing in tighter on both sides. We're really going off-road now. The taillights flare every so often, as he slows to navigate around a large rock or deep pothole. I have to be careful, too. Following in the dark wake, I could easily twist an ankle.

For ten minutes we crawl onward, the track getting steadily rougher. He's taking me to Emma. I can just feel it. I must work out a plan for when he finds her. The odds are no better than before, two against one. I'll have Emma on my side, and she's a good fighter, so I've been told. That depends, however, on what state she's in. God knows what they've already done to her before she escaped. This time, however, I'll have the element of surprise, not them. Either Pritchard and the woman are going to die, or Emma and I are. It's the last stand.

After fifteen more minutes, the Jeep pulls off onto a small sealed road and speeds up.

Crap!

I take off after it, running as fast as I can, keeping it in sight. The taillights flare again, and thankfully it slows. The beam of the headlights angle to the right, and the Jeep pulls into a small unlit parking lot, like a picnic area.

I keep back and watch as the headlights cut out, plunging everything into darkness. Then the internal light winks on, and they climb out. They move off together, Pritchard leading the way along a set path, a flashlight in his hand. The flashlight slowly fades, and they're gone into a wall of black.

They're on foot, can't drive anymore, and following a proper trail. But where?

I run past the parked Jeep and slip my cell phone out, then turn on the flashlight, covering the screen with my fingers so I get just enough light to see where I'm going but not enough light to give me away. They have disappeared along the path, but I'll catch up.

A wooden sign materializes out of the gloom, next to the entrance of a trailhead. I read the words carved into the plank of wood next to an arrow: *Slaughter Falls 700 yds*. Aptly named. But why would Emma be there? And, more importantly, how do they know Emma is there? They're not searching anymore. They are now following a hiker's trail to the waterfall as though they know where they're going, like someone will be waiting for them at the end.

A rendezvous.

None of it makes sense. Making sense of anything when it comes to Pritchard, I gave up on a long time ago.

There's barely enough moonlight, but it's going to have to do. Turning off my phone's flashlight, I enter the trail, and instantly it feels like I'm walking into some deep fissure below the earth's crust.

The road to hell.

45

IT'S TIME

Her ankle throbbed, and coldness crept across her skin, making her shiver.

Emma knew when she saw the trail sign that it was the perfect spot. She had found it on a map signboard she had discovered on a hiking trail she had stumbled across, dispelling the notion that she was, in fact, now in a sprawling state forest and not some small patch of woodland.

The map signboard showed in intricate detail the various long and short hiking paths, and after straining her eyes, staring at the map, she had chosen the perfect location to draw Pritchard and Dolly to her. While it had been a test of her stamina, with her ankle, to trek up to the lookout point right next to the waterfall, it was worth it. As well as having the advantage of securing the higher ground, she could see them coming well before they would see her.

After she arrived at the parking lot, she followed the hiking trail that wound its way through the woods, climbing higher and higher, until it eventually led to a viewing platform set on huge, flat slabs of monolithic stone, next to the edge of a waterfall. A deep channel of brooding dark forest below stretched into the distance. A constant sheet of water slid over the edge of the waterfall and out of sight, plunging a hundred feet into the darkness below, before echoing back the dull crash of the water smashing upon the rocks. A cloud of misty spray, caught in the uninterrupted glare of the moon, rose, shimmering and translucent, in a silvery haze, from the base of the waterfall.

Her ankle had throbbed during the hike, making her think she must have snagged it on a fallen tree branch when she had sloshed ankle-deep through a thick layer of leaves and forest debris somewhere in the woods. She was feeling dizzy, too, swinging between bouts where her skin felt hot and clammy, then icy with a cold sweat as it did now. What she was wearing was definitely not suitable for the change in temperature of being outside. *Maybe I'm just dehydrated*, Emma thought, pushing aside how she felt and concentrating on what she had to do next, to draw Pritchard and Dolly here, to this exact location, right on the edge of the waterfall.

Dolly was already injured with her jaw, and Emma was confident she could take her. It was Pritchard, however, who presented the bigger problem. Martial arts skills can be easily overrated. No match for the sheer size and blunt force that Pritchard presented. He also had a gun, taken from the corpse of the ranger. A pang of sadness welled up inside her as she thought about him, and the father and daughter.

Emma's hastily prepared plan involved grabbing Dolly first, using her as a human shield, and threatening to plunge the steel spike into the artery of her neck if Pritchard didn't give her the keys to the Jeep, *and* the gun, too. And if he wouldn't give her the gun as well? Then she would force him to toss it into the falls below. She would then run back to the Jeep, drive off, and get help. Was it the perfect plan? No plan was ever perfect, and plenty could go wrong with hers. She was determined to fight for her life.

She stood on the edge of the rocky plateau, her back to the void of the valley below, waiting for them to appear and trying to swallow the nerves she felt. It was the only plan she had.

This was her last stand.

Emma saw the swaying beam of a funnel of light filtering through the trees in the distance, well back from the start of the path that led out of the forest and into the viewing area.

She tensed, one hand by her side banging her thigh in a nervous twitch. Like a lantern atop a miner's helmet as he ducked and weaved through a tunnel, the funnel of light ducked and weaved its way toward Emma, following the path she had taken herself.

Then the beam of light abruptly vanished. The woods again assumed their impenetrable blackness.

Cold, bony fingers scraped along Emma's spine.

Stay calm. You can do this.

Then came the thud of footsteps, slow and deliberate. They grew louder. Emma imagined his heavy work boots coming toward her. Scuffed and scarred, the leather skin of one toe slit open.

She bunched her hands into tight fists.

Time's up. The wait was over.

They were here.

Let the fun and games begin.

46

FATAL MISTAKE

Don't fear what you can't see. A line Emma had read somewhere, and most likely her next tattoo if she got out of here alive, that is, entered her mind as she peered into the darkness, unable to see anything.

The shadows parted, and the hulking shape of Pritchard materialized first, followed by Dolly.

Emma's breath caught as fear crushed one of her lungs, rendering it useless, making her feel like she was breathing with only the other.

Stay calm. Stay calm. Remember the plan. You can do it. Her fingers were bunched so tightly into fists, she thought her knuckles might pop out from under the thin skin.

The moon, full and blanched, bathed everything in a watery glow, making both Pritchard's and Dolly's faces as drawn and gaunt as skulls, their eye sockets deep and dark. They stopped and regarded her.

Emma kept her feet firmly planted where they were. Another foot back, and she would topple over the ledge, her body sailing out into the abyss before smashing onto rocks at the base of the waterfall below.

It was Dolly who moved first, stepping forward, leaving Pritchard in the background. "Well, well, well," her crooked, puppetlike jaw gibbered up and down. "Look what we have here."

Emma kept her hands by her sides and slightly behind her.

Dolly's face creased. She turned back to Pritchard, who was standing a few feet behind her. "How did you know she was here?"

Emma watched Pritchard, trying to gauge his reaction. His eyes remained on her, as they had when he had first seen her. Silent and motionless, it was almost as if he hadn't heard Dolly's question.

So she was clueless about his little game, Emma thought. Planting the tracking chip inside the penknife, then innocently leaving it behind for her to cut the ropes that bound her. Missing her twice in his pickup after driving like a maniac and killing the father and daughter, then the ranger. Then driving off in the Jeep, knowing full well she was hiding under its chassis.

Pritchard finally spoke. "Intuition, I guess."

Dolly didn't seem convinced. "What do you mean, intuition?"

Emma could detect a certain cynicism in the woman's voice. She wasn't buying it.

Pritchard stepped forward, his eyes never leaving Emma's. "Like I said before, I had a feeling she'd be up here, or at least somewhere around here in the woods."

Another wave of dizziness came over Emma. She teetered slightly, then swallowed. It was almost like she had vertigo, but she had never been afraid of heights before. And when she had first arrived at the spot, she had looked down over the edge of the cliff and felt nothing.

Sweat beaded on her forehead. Cold, wet little blisters, as though frozen ants were crawling over her face. Fearing she might topple backward, she took a few steps forward, away from the edge. A tight noose of pain choked her left ankle, and she almost stumbled.

Dolly was still turned toward Pritchard, and she missed Emma's stumble. But Pritchard hadn't. He lifted his head a few inches. His eyes, glinting like wet coal, seemed to grow as he regarded Emma.

Dolly, apparently satisfied with Pritchard's explanation, turned back to Emma. "Come away from the edge, honey." Her voice moist and sticky. "It would be such a pity if you should fall by accident."

Shifting most of her weight to her right foot, Emma took another step forward. *What's wrong with me?* Her skin felt hot and prickly despite the cold air being carried aloft from the base of the waterfall. Why was she feeling hot? She looked at Dolly and blinked. Now there were three of her. Triplets, all fuzzy and overlaid.

Dolly took a step forward and held out her hand. "Come here."

"Don't come any closer. Or I'll jump!" Emma warned, her eyes shifting in and out of focus.

Dolly tilted her head. "And why would you do a stupid thing like that?"

"Can't keep running," Emma said, looking directly at Dolly. "Do what you want to me then let me go. Or I'll jump. Killing myself is a better way to go, on my own terms." That was the plan; first appeal to Dolly's depravity. Give the woman a slither of hope that she would get what she's always wanted. Her. Emma caressed one of her breasts, rubbing the nipple through the fabric of her crop top. "You want me, don't you?"

Mesmerized, Dolly's eyes dropped to where Emma's fingers were stroking, teasing, twisting. She licked her lips. Practically salivating at what she was seeing.

"Jump, then," Pritchard called out. "That's if you've got the guts to. See if I care."

Dolly flew into a panic, and her hands went up in protest. "No! No! No!" She edged closer to Emma. "That would be such a waste, my dear. Let me have you, then I'll let you go."

Pritchard shifted uncomfortably, then took a few steps forward. "Dolly," he warned. "What are you doing?"

Emma shot a look at Pritchard, saw the look of icy disdain. He wasn't happy with Dolly's proposal. Her jumping to her death would spoil his plans. But was he bluffing? Did he really not care if she jumped or not? Emma had no intention of jumping. *Two can play at this game.*

Dolly took another step forward. "I'm sure we can come to an agreement. Like you said, let me have my way with you, and I promise, you have my word, that I will let you go."

"What about him?" Emma countered, nodding toward Pritchard. In the moonlight, his face had turned to stone. Good, she thought. This will ruin his plans.

"Dolly," Pritchard warned again, his voice firmer this time. "That's not what we agreed on."

Without turning, Dolly waved a dismissive hand. "Forget what we discussed," she snapped. "Do you think I'm stupid? I don't know how, but you knew she would be here."

Pritchard's jaw seemed to bulge.

"Don't worry about him, honey," Dolly continued. "Give me your hand. You'll be fine. I promise."

Emma slumped her shoulders and bowed her head in defeat.

Dolly stepped forward to within arm's reach of Emma, the fingers of her outstretched hand beckoning her.

Emma took her hand. It was as sweaty and as pudgy as unbaked dough.

"That's my girl," Dolly cooed. "And yes, dear. You are *my* girl. No one else's."

Emma's fingers closed over Dolly's hand, securing the grip.

Dolly's body went limp, relenting, as Emma pulled her into an embrace—then brought her right hand up with speed, the sharp steel spike protruded between her fingers, the penknife wrapped tightly in her fist. Like a sewing machine needle driving at full tilt, Emma's fist blurred as she delivered a flurry of short, sharp jabs, the steel spike stitching deep, bloody punctures across Dolly's face and throat.

Screaming, Dolly went to pull away, but Emma held her hand tightly, increasing the speed and ferocity of her spiked punches. Haunting images blinded Emma's vision: the pink miniature tea set, the fragment of skull all wrapped in a bloodied tuft of strawberry blonde hair, the mangled remains of the father, the dead park ranger, and the last twenty-four hours of living hell she had to endure under the constant threat of dying a cruel, sexually sadistic death. It all came flooding back to her and was as though her brain had tapped into some deep, primitive reservoir of survival hormone that was now surging through her veins, feeding her tired muscles and depleted willpower, giving her a newfound strength and stamina.

Dolly brought her hand up, trying desperately to protect her face, and Emma instantly shifted the angle of her attack, raining looping right hooks around Dolly's arm, driving the spike repeatedly into the side of Dolly's head, her face looking like she had smashed it repeatedly into a bed of nails.

Dolly sank to her knees, and Emma followed her down. Leaning over her, she began punching the top of her head: her spiked fist moving back and forth like a downward piston.

Exhausted, Emma finally let go, and Dolly collapsed headfirst into the hard rock.

It was a change in plan. Emma never intended to do what she had just done. She planned to hold the spike against Dolly's throat like a hostage, convince Pritchard to give her the keys to the Jeep. Then she lost it, triggered by Dolly's insatiable hunger to hurt and abuse her. *Never again.*

She looked up, her chest heaving from the exertion, her right hand gloved in blood. Dolly's blood.

During the entire duration of the attack, ten seconds by Emma's estimate, Pritchard hadn't moved. Not an inch. Now he just stood there looking at her with what she thought was a smile on his face.

It was then Emma realized she had made a fatal mistake.

47

FINISH HER

"Finish her," Pritchard growled, his voice low and gravelly, his eyes hooded.

What? Emma glanced down to where Dolly lay at her feet, blood pooling under her, dark and viscous as crude oil in the moonlight. The woman was making wet, wheezing sounds through the puncture holes in her throat in between incoherent sobs and moans.

Glancing back up, Emma saw a wicked, twisted smile spreading across Pritchard's face. She could have sworn he was getting some kind of sexual arousal from the whole incident. Now she understood. He wanted this. That's why he had stood back, did nothing, just watched while Emma made a human pincushion out of Dolly's head, face, and neck.

"I said, finish her," he said, this time stepping forward, his voice sounding like it was swimming up from the depths of a deep tomb.

Emma was no killer. She wasn't that ruthless. Dolly was injured, most likely fatally if left to bleed out. But she would not slit her throat like an injured deer or elk. Did she feel sorry for the woman? Absolutely not. She got what she deserved.

Emma threw down the bloodied penknife. "No." The small knife would be useless against him. She couldn't defend herself against him with a much larger breadknife and now the element of surprise was lost.

Despite Pritchard's perverse smile, Emma saw death in his eyes, long and lingering death.

"If you finish her, I'll be quick with you, little lady," he said. "It'll be painless."

"And if I don't?"

"Then I'll take weeks, not days, with you."

What sort of deal was that? "Why don't you finish her?" Emma sneered, lifting her chin defiantly.

Pritchard inhaled deeply, then slowly nodded. "You know why. It's a game, and you're playing it whether you like it or not."

His words confirmed what Emma had figured out. It *was* a game. A game that he controlled, where death, slow and painful, was the only prize on offer.

"And you need to earn your quick death," he continued. "There's nothing else. No freedom. No life. Just death. That's all I'm offering you. But you must earn it. Such a privilege comes at a cost."

Emma couldn't believe what she was hearing. Kill Dolly so that she could earn a quick, humane death? He truly was a cruel and twisted son of a bitch.

"Fuck you!" Emma gave her answer before another wave of dizziness gripped her. She wobbled slightly, and everything was thrown out of focus. Her ankle was throbbing much worse now.

"Fuck you?" Pritchard said, mimicking Emma's response. "I must congratulate you, however, on finding the tracker. Credit where credit is due."

"Why? Why didn't you just kill me when you had the chance?" Emma asked.

Pritchard bowed his head slightly at her. "Again, you know the answer to that."

It was almost like his dark eyes were penetrating into her mind, reading her thoughts.

"A quick death," Pritchard repeated. "Or I promise you a slow and painful one." Then, as if to entice her, he added, "And no one will ever know what happened to you. I'll bury you deep. Really deep. Think of all the pain and anguish it would reap on your family. Not knowing what happened to you."

Emma felt her anger bristling. Not knowing. No closure. It would destroy her mother and most likely her father, too, whom she hadn't met. It would be like condemning them to an eternity of suffering as well. One last act of cruelty that was so unimaginable. Her parents would be roped into an endless living nightmare.

"But if you finish what you started, killing her now..." Pritchard said. "Do this for me, and I promise they will find your body. Give you a proper burial."

To Emma, it was sounding like a rehearsed speech from Pritchard, leaving her to wonder how many women he had made the same offer to. He was the devil seated at hell's poker table, dealing out nothing but death cards.

Emma's vision came back into focus. "Toss away the gun, then," she said. "And I'll do it."

Pritchard lifted his jaw and studied Emma for a moment.

"Like you said," she continued, "it's a game. You knew I was under the Jeep, and I saw you take the gun from the ranger. I'll kill Dolly, but you and I get to face off after that." The idea had just come to her. She needed to appeal to Pritchard's hunting desires. At least she might stand a better chance. She stepped forward, challenging him. "Just the two of us. No weapons. Right now. The ultimate finale to your game. Winner gets to live, and the loser..." She let the words trail off.

Pritchard inhaled deeply, and she could see he was thinking about it.

"If you really *are* a true hunter," she added, "then you also need to earn my death."

A ravenous smile spread across his face, and Emma knew immediately she had triggered something primal deep inside him. He slipped the gun from his waistband at the small of his back and tossed it high over Emma's head and out over the edge where it vanished into the darkness.

Emma nodded. "Good. Now it's just you and me." Then something caught her eye behind Pritchard. A flutter of movement in the background, the shadows suddenly shifting and moving.

Pritchard saw the shift in Emma's attention and turned to look behind him.

48

FALLING

It was a sound Emma would never forget, like a watermelon hitting the sidewalk after being dropped from the top of the Empire State Building.

She watched as Pritchard's head jolted violently sideways, while his feet remained firmly planted on the ground. A high-pitched shrill cut through the darkness, and a woman appeared from behind Pritchard. She had been obscured from Emma's view by his bulk.

Wide-eyed and manic, her mouth drawn open in a rictus grin, she screamed like a banshee, then delivered another blow to Pritchard's head with the rock, black and glistening, she held aloft in her hand. Then another wet, melon-bursting crack, harder and louder, bashing his head to one side as though it were attached to a spring. A human bobblehead.

This time Pritchard moved. He staggered back and began swaying drunkenly, still refusing to go down.

Smack! Another skull-crunching blow to the head. Another step backward by him away from the onslaught.

Then another blow, and another.

He staggered sideways this time, retreating away from Emma along the rocky ledge but not before she caught a glimpse of his face.

Resembling a scrunched-up ball of paper, one side of his face was caved in. Grotesque and sunken, it was a mushy red mask of bludgeoned flesh and shattered bone.

Relentlessly, the woman, a stranger to Emma, continued playing Whac-A-Mole, the arcade game, with Pritchard's skull, deftly stepping across the slabs of flat rock like they were lily pads, in pursuit of him. Matching him step for step, the woman doggedly stalked Pritchard as he staggered and stumbled over the layers of flat rock. She would wait for him to lose balance, raise the rock, then smash it down on his head. It was a wonder he hadn't collapsed under the brutal storm of blows she was raining down on him.

Emma went to move, when fingers seemed to rise out of the earth near her feet, a corpse coming back to life, and grabbed her swollen ankle. She screamed out in pain.

The woman attacking Pritchard stopped momentarily and turned toward Emma, the rock poised in her hand for another blow. She seemed to hesitate, teetering with indecision. She glanced back at Pritchard, who was hobbling away, then back at Emma, before pursuing Pritchard again with a renewed sense of urgency.

Looking down, Emma saw Dolly, weepy-eyed and bloodied, looking back up at her. A watery, gelatinous blob, the remains of one of Dolly's punctured eyeballs, oozed from its socket. Resembling a soft, cut egg yolk, it slid down her cheek like a slug escaping from a muddy red hole.

Shrieking, Emma tried pulling her leg away, but Dolly clung to her ankle, anchoring her in place. Her sheer mass no comparison to Emma's lighter frame.

Wet, raspy noises whistled from Dolly's mouth and neck. Using Emma's leg as a ladder, she began slowly creeping up from the ground. Hand over hand, first Emma's ankle, then up to her shin, and finally around her thigh, Dolly pulled herself up gradually.

Waves of burning pain spread from Emma's ankle and up her leg. Refusing to give up, she started punching Dolly in the sides of her head with her fists, regretting that she had thrown away the penknife.

The blows seemed to have no effect. Dolly was on her knees now, her jaw dangling on stretched skin. Reaching up, she grabbed at Emma's chest, cruel fingers digging into her breasts, blood and spittle flicking up into Emma's face as she snarled like a rabid dog.

Then Dolly was on her feet, hunched like some demented sloth, blood oozing from a multitude of puncture holes in her face and throat. Both her hands dug into Emma's arms, and she began shunting Emma backward, sumo-wrestler style toward the edge.

Hot, delirious, and weak, Emma could do nothing but slide back one foot at a time. The soles of her sneakers, worn smooth by constant use, provided little resistance on the flat rock surface. Looking around wildly, Emma saw Pritchard at the very edge of the cliff, sheets of water sluicing off into space next to him. The woman was holding the rock high above her head threateningly, Pritchard on his knees now, cowering.

Dolly gave Emma another shove, pushing her farther toward the edge.

Glancing over her shoulder, Emma saw that there was no escape. A few more feet, and she would plunge to her death on the rocks below.

Again, Emma looked over to where the woman was standing and cried out to her.

The woman turned and looked toward Emma, her hand still raised, ready to bring the rock crashing down on Pritchard's skull in a final, mortal blow.

Dolly pushed Emma again.

I CAN REACH her in time. I can save her. That evil woman is there. Shoving Emma toward the edge.

I turn back to see Pritchard—gone? No, wait. He's on his hands and knees, crawling away from me, maybe ten feet from me now. The bastard skulked off while I was looking away.

Another scream by Emma. I turn toward her. She's so close to the edge.

It's her or Pritchard. Only seconds left for me to make a choice.

I drop the rock and start running toward Emma, praying that I can reach her in time.

No! No! No! She's falling.

Memento mori. Remember, you must die.

DOLLY GAVE ANOTHER PUSH, and Emma's heels slid out over the ledge.

Her body weight shifted, and she could feel herself toppling backward. She began flailing her arms, trying to grab at the air to pull herself forward. Her fingers found something, and she latched on to it. It was Dolly's sleeve. Her backward tilt halted—until the rock under one of her feet crumbled and fell away.

With one foot on the edge, and one hand holding on to Dolly's sleeve, Emma tilted back again.

"Die, you fucking bitch!" Dolly croaked, her one remaining eye swiveling like a cyclops. Bringing her opposite hand up, she started twisting each of Emma's fingers off her sleeve, one by one.

"No!" Emma cried, tightening her grip on the material of the sleeve, feeling it tear.

One finger, then two, came away.

"Bye, bye," Dolly sneered.

A third finger came away.

"Have a pleasant fligh—" Dolly's head was suddenly wrenched back.

A hand shot out to Emma. As powerful and as determined as an eagle's claw, it latched on to her wrist and ripped her body back to safety.

Emma collapsed onto her back, the reassuring feel of solid ground beneath her. Then she heard the whiplash crack of the bones breaking in Dolly's neck before seeing Dolly's body sail out over the edge and disappear from view.

Half-dazed and ravaged by a feverish heat, Emma looked up to see a woman's face staring down at her. The same woman she had seen smashing Pritchard with the rock. "Th-than-thank you," Emma stuttered before she passed out.

EMMA'S SAFE! Crouching, I pull her to me, cradling her in my arms. She's burning up, like she has a fever. I hold her close. "Oh, baby, I've got you. I've got you." I rock her slowly, tears welling in my eyes.

Emma murmurs something I can't decipher, and I hug her tighter. "It's okay, baby. It's going to be okay. You're safe."

Turning, I look up toward where I last saw Pritchard.

He's gone.

I turn my attention back to Emma. God, she looks so young, so frail in my arms. Her skin tastes of dirt and salty sweat as I kiss her forehead. "You are a fighter," I say, rocking her gently. Holding her close with one arm, I slip out my cell phone and start calling everyone as tears of frustration and joy roll down my cheeks.

Pritchard is gone. The woman is dead. Emma is safe.

49

PENANCE

I don't usually kill women, but I made an exception in her case.

She's dead and I'm happy I killed her. I considered it self-defense. Luckily for me, they concluded her broken neck was likely the result of the fall. That and the fact that no one can survive a hundred-foot drop headfirst into a pile of rocks. Emma might remember what really happened after I saved her. It's a risk I'm willing to take.

There are three of us sitting in a windowless interview room Camilla PD kindly lent us. While Aaron Wood looks thoroughly pissed that I betrayed his trust, Dan Miller, an old FBI colleague, who was once my partner at the bureau, seems more pragmatic. Miller was with me in Utah when we had Pritchard cornered, only to have him escape. He's almost as determined as I am to find him. Wood is, too, but he's not a field agent. He wouldn't understand.

Miller doesn't take things personally. Wood, on the other hand, like a petulant child, is silently seething at me as though I sent him to the naughty corner. It's baffled him how I, all on my own, and with a little help from Beatriz Vega, managed to find Pritchard while the combined might, power, and resources of the FBI couldn't.

Roadblocks were set up, local as well as state police were mobilized, and Aaron Wood and Dan Miller were en route with a contingent of agents within the hour after I called. And somehow, as I expected, Pritchard, despite the injuries he must have sustained, slipped through and vanished. DNA taken from blood on the rock and at the scene confirmed it was him. There was nothing else of value that was found in the cabin or the fallout shelter. The FBI, however, are still exploring the network of tunnels, and according to Miller, are following up on if there are any stolen vehicles from nearby properties that border the state forest.

Twenty-four hours on and still no sign of him. He's long gone, I imagine. Slinking off like an injured creature, back under a rock or into a hole in the ground. I doubt if he will present himself at an ER. But the authorities are checking on them all within a fifty-mile radius. Despite the horrific injuries I had inflicted on him, that would have killed any normal human being, Pritchard wasn't normal or human. He was still alive. I could almost hear his black heart beating somewhere in my subconscious.

"How's Emma doing?" I ask, shifting from the topic that has dominated the conversation for the last hour: Samuel Pritchard.

"She's fine," Miller replies. "The paramedics were quick to give her the snake antivenom. She'll be out of the hospital in a few days."

"She was lucky."

Miller nods. "Yeah. She thought she had snagged her ankle on a hidden branch that was buried under some leaves. Thought nothing of it."

I had thought at the time that she was burning up because of a fever or because of the hot-blooded survival state she had been subjected to.

"So, I've told you all I know about Sam Pritchard," I say. Well, not everything. "What can you tell me about the woman with him?"

Miller pulls another folder and opens it. "Her name is Dolores Edith Gruber, sixty-two. She also goes by the names of Calma Lafary, Edith Grayson, and Dolores Jobert. She's a sexual sadist who targets young girls to groom into sexual slaves."

"Sounds like a very nasty piece of work," I say.

Miller flips a page. "That's not the half of it. She's been running from authorities for nearly three years now. Six charges of rape involving penetration. Indecent sexual assault of minors as young as twelve. Sexual torture. Kidnapping. Sexual assault."

"How did she find them?" I glance at Aaron. Like a sentinel he remains silent, just watching me. He'll get over it. I just don't think he enjoyed being showed up in front of his peers by a solitary ex-FBI agent who is now a humble civilian.

Miller continues. "In the past, she's posed as a schoolteacher. A girl's camp counselor. A volunteer at a single mothers' shelter. And a nurse at a drug rehabilitation clinic for young women, just to name a few."

"All giving her unfettered access to vulnerable girls and young women." My revulsion for Dolores Gruber reaches an all-time high—so does my happiness that I killed her.

"Absolutely. She's also posed several times as an officer from the Department of Family and Protective Services in several states, including Texas and Maryland. She kidnapped four girls separately, kept them in a converted room in her basement, sexually assaulting them for weeks. When she was done, she drugged them and dumped them on the side of the road. One girl, an eight-year-old, is still missing."

"Christ," I murmur. "Some pedophile was probably driving past and thought it was Christmas." What I did to Gruber now seems like a suitable penance for all her abhorrent sins.

"Most likely." Miller closes the file. "Gruber would do anything and everything to get access to young girls. She had an insatiable appetite for sexually assaulting them."

"Do you have any idea how they met?" I ask. "Her and Pritchard?"

"No idea," Miller replies. "I guess birds of a feather flock together and all that. Sick bastards attract each other. They congregate, like how they do online. I imagine that's how they met. Or on the road, even. Caught each other staring at the same vulnerable young woman."

Something's burning inside me. Something I want to ask when the time is right. It will devastate me if I get the answer I don't want.

Then, as if he knows what I'm thinking, Miller says, "And no. Gruber didn't sexually assault Emma."

Thank God. Joy springs eternally inside me.

I sit back and stare out a window that only I can see. Through it, I see Dolores Gruber on a constant loop, flying through the air before smashing into the rocks at the base of the waterfall. I smile.

"What's so funny?" Wood asks, a sour look on his face.

"Oh, nothing. Bonnie and Clyde maybe. I didn't know that Pritchard had teamed up with someone." I tap the table. "But you're right, Dan. They probably met online or somewhere on the road. Crossed each other's path and recognized a shared interest in debauchery and evil."

"That seems like the logical explanation," Wood chimes in again. Anger simmers somewhere behind his eyes. Now it's developed into a staring competition between the two of us.

"As you know, Carolyn," Miller interjects, clearing his throat. "Pritchard never sexually abused any of his victims."

Wood breaks eye contact first and looks down at his notebook.

I guess I win. "It's not his style," I say, picking up Miller's ball and running with it. My eyes linger a while longer on Wood before I address Miller. "His need is murder—and torture—to a certain degree. But sexual abuse, remarkably, has never appealed to him." I pause when it hits me. "That's interesting."

Miller is smiling at me, nodding his head, encouraging me to go on. It's just like the good old days between us. Midnight in some empty diner. On the side of a dirt road near a cornfield. Or at a gas station, drinking bad coffee and eating stale doughnuts. The two of us, comparing case notes, witness statements, crime scene photos. A tinge of loneliness pangs in my chest.

"That's how their relationship flourished," I continue. I see it in Miller's eyes, too, while Wood is still sulking. He'll get over it.

"They complemented each other." Miller nods.

Totally. "It sounds disgusting, but they weren't competing. They were simply sharing the one victim to satisfy their own individual but separate needs."

"It doesn't sound disgusting," Wood quips, with more than a hint of animosity in his voice. I'm not sure if it's directed at me or Pritchard and Gruber.

"It is barbaric," he adds.

A thin smile forms on my lips as I address him. "And Gruber wasn't on your radar?"

Wood glances at Miller, who gives a nod.

"We've been tracking her for a while," Wood continues. "Assisting with local and state law enforcement when they asked for our help a few months back."

"But we did not know she had teamed up with Pritchard," Miller says.

We say nothing for a few moments, and I think about what has happened. I could have not killed Dolores Gruber. I could have subdued her until the police came. Then we would have had all the answers to our questions—if she complied, that is. Maybe even the location of where Pritchard may have fled to. His shelter. Creatures like Pritchard always have a refuge they run to when it all hits the fan, and they need to lie low for a while.

In that moment, however, rage had consumed me. Rage at having to let Pritchard go, to save Emma. Rage at Gruber for trying to kill Emma. Rage at the world that life right now for me isn't fair.

Thankfully, in the heat of battle, I chose the cleanest, most logical way of killing her that would cause minimal blowback for me.

"Carolyn."

"Carolyn?"

"What?" I glance up to see both staring at me. It's like time ticked on for a few minutes without me.

"You look miles away," Miller says.

Suddenly, I feel like I'm about to throw up. My eyes lose focus, and the small interview room spins. I grip the edge of the table and the spinning slows.

"Carolyn, what's the matter?" I hear Miller asking. Looking up, I see just two fuzzy outlines sitting across from me. "N-nothing."

Reaching for a glass of water, I just manage to find my mouth and take a gulp while trying to stop my hand from shaking. Slowly, the spinning stops, the nausea passes, and my eyes come back into focus. I reach up to touch the side of my head, then pause and quickly retract my hand. Part of my left cheek is numb.

"Are you sure you are fine?" Wood asks, concern in his face. He fills up my glass and slides it back to me.

I blink hard. "I'm fine. Sorry. Just the strain of the last few days."

"Are you sure you are okay?" Miller touches my hand. "We can continue this some other time."

I wave him off. "No. Let's get it over and done with." I take another sip of water, and out of the corner of my eye, I see them exchange looks. "Most likely low blood sugar as well," I add, thinking back to the stack of pecan pancakes, topped with bacon, and drizzled with maple syrup that I devoured two hours ago at breakfast. I hadn't eaten in almost two days.

I wipe my mouth with a napkin. Whatever it was is gone now. It was as if I had glimpsed death rushing behind my eyes before it spirited away to claim someone else.

Now I am worried. Will I be able to finish what I have started? Can I do this on my own? The simple answer is a resounding yes. Until my last breath, I will keep searching for Pritchard until I find him again and kill him.

Wood and Miller are both eyeing me suspiciously. "Let's keep going," I insist.

Miller checks his file while Wood is just looking at me. I force myself to think of something, a place, a time when I was the happiest. It's a trick I've learned over the years, when I need to focus on the good and not the bad. Or when I'm feeling particularly low or depressed. It also comes in handy, like right now, when I need to put a genuine smile on my face instead of a false one. And Wood and Miller are both two highly skilled interrogators. Especially Miller. They will know if I am faking it.

So, I think of Ben. And just like that, bang!

"What else?" I ask, with a smile.

50

ALONE

"What I don't get," Aaron Wood asks, "is what made you stop at that particular gas station in the first place?"

"Like I've already told you. I flew to Columbus, then drove to see Karen Block, Emma's mother, about her daughter's disappearance." So far, I've kept Vega out of the conversation and intend to continue to do so. She's the only external resource I have, and her anonymity must be protected at all costs. I cannot do this without her. She is my lifeline. There is no way I'm going to tell them that Vega had hacked into the FBI database, let alone the security cameras at the gas station, which revealed that Pritchard in his black pickup truck had been there.

"And just after the meeting, I needed gas. The gas station I just chanced upon. That was all."

Wood doesn't look convinced. He hasn't looked convinced of anything I've said for the entire meeting.

"And you just happened to be talking to one of the servers at the diner. A woman called Frances Pridmore, who told you about a fallout shelter near a log cabin?"

This is sounding more like an interrogation from Wood.

"Like I said before. I made inquiries of anyone and everyone around the town about Emma's disappearance. Local police didn't seem to care." I bet they're caring now. Caring about how to best cover their collective asses. "There's no law against that."

"You just took it upon yourself," Wood continues, "even though you told me specifically that you weren't going after Pritchard."

I shrug. "You forget. I don't work for the FBI anymore. I can do what I damn well want."

Right away the air in the small room thickens, like an uncrossable gulf of water has sprung up between us. The mention of Frances saddens me. Her funeral will be in a few days. I will pay my respects, as I will also do when I attend the funerals of the father and daughter, and the law enforcement ranger who was also murdered by Pritchard.

"And why Emma Block?" Wood asks, his eyes narrowing. "Why was she so special?"

I give another shrug. Her case file was initially on his radar, as a missing person, and likely a victim of Pritchard's. Then he dismissed it. "She was a missing person who fit the profile," I say.

"What profile?" Wood demands.

"My profile." I lean forward. "I am more than capable of creating my own victimology based on Pritchard's past victims. After all, I believe I know him better than anyone else."

Wood bristles at my comments. Perhaps it's got something to do with his ego being dented. I have an ego, too. Bigger than most. But I put it to good use in apprehending monsters like Pritchard.

Wood throws me a skeptical look. "So, you troll through possibly hundreds of missing-persons reports each day, trying to find a match of Pritchard's next potential victim?"

I glance at Miller. He looks like he's interested to know the answer to the question, too.

"What can I say? I have a lot of spare time on my hands."

Miller smirks, but Wood still isn't convinced. Does he suspect his files have been hacked? I doubt it. If either he or Miller knew, I wouldn't be sitting here at this present moment. I'd be manacled and chained, sitting in a jail cell. So would Beatriz Vega. There is still time for that, too. If I slip up.

"And this Frances Pridmore just volunteered the information to you?" Wood asks.

He's trying to poke holes in my statements. I'm not lying. Just withholding some finer details. "Like I said before, it's more granular, my approach. Being on the ground, talking to the locals, seeing what I can see. You can't do that sitting in an office in Virginia." I can't help shooting that barb at him. He is a bit of an office hermit, a lab rat.

Something flares behind Wood's eyes, like he's been stung by a wasp. Good. He hasn't seen what I've seen. He sees the aftermath. The cold, pallid aftermath of the violence. He is not there in real time when the killing starts as it did. He didn't see the remains of that poor father and his daughter, smashed like roadkill, just moments after it happened. The blood, still warm and wet. The smell of fresh flesh still lingering. He didn't hear the sickening sound of Frances Pridmore's neck being snapped like a chicken's, right in front of him.

Miller raises his hand, trying to stop the battle that is brewing across the table between Aaron Wood and me.

"Carolyn," he says. "We have agents on the ground, too."

"I know, Dan. I was one of them, remember? But we all look like agents. People aren't that forthcoming when they see us coming, like an army of matching suits with badges around our necks and guns on our hips." The image of an army of Mr. Smiths from *The Matrix*, all marching in unison, comes to mind.

Miller makes an expression that tells me he agrees with my candid assessment of how the FBI is construed by the public at large.

"I'm nimbler," I confess. "People talk to me; they answer my questions." I look down at my clothes: a pair of jeans and a crumpled polo shirt I had stashed in the back seat of my rental car. "I look less intimidating. People open up to me because I look like one of them, and I talk like one of them." That doesn't mean to say people didn't open up to me when I was an agent wearing a badge and carrying a gun on my hip. I just have a different approach now, more empathy. Before, while I was a fed, I was all gung-ho and kicking in doors, treating everyone like a suspect. I've mellowed a bit. Only a bit.

Then Wood rolls out the howitzer, takes aim, and fires. I knew it was a possibility, his ulterior motive, hidden for almost the entire length of the meeting. I just didn't think he would be so harsh, so scathing.

"You could be charged in Georgia with hindering the apprehension or the punishment of a criminal," he states.

I twist my mouth and grit my teeth.

He continues, "You could go to jail for up to five years. You should've called the killings in as soon as you discovered them. You shouldn't have delayed. You have a moral and legal responsibility when you witness a murder, to call the authorities." He sits back almost proudly before throwing a sharp little barb. "Even if you are *just* a civilian now."

As tempting as it is to remind him that I found Pritchard, not him, while he had at his disposal millions of taxpayers' dollars, I refrain. Such petty point-scoring isn't me.

I look at Miller. His silence speaks volumes. Perhaps it's me and not Pritchard who truly frightens them more.

Before the silence becomes unbearable, Miller speaks again, his voice calming and soothing. "Let's not get ahead of ourselves." Then he addresses me. "But Aaron is right, Carolyn. If the authorities here in Georgia decide to take it upon themselves to charge you, and they have more than ample grounds to do so, from what you have told us, then we can't intervene. You'll be on your own."

I smile, then say, "Being alone is a gift that not everyone has the strength or the balls to fully appreciate."

51

TWO MONTHS LATER
THE GIRL THAT GOT AWAY

The sting of the needle was painful. But now she could tolerate much more pain than she ever could before.

The needle paused, and the soft shrill of a buzzing mosquito stopped. A small piece of gauze wiped away the pinpricks of blood oozing from the skin on the inside of her forearm.

Sitting in the leather chair, she looked down and smiled, admiring the artistry.

"How does it look so far?" the man wearing black nitrile gloves asked. The scaled twist of a dragon's tail accented in green, yellow, and red seemed to slither up one side of his neck as he turned his head toward the woman.

"Perfect."

The woman watched on as the mosquito buzzing started up again, and the needle resumed its repeated piercing, pushing ink pigment into the top layers of her skin. The design, a small mammal with powerful haunches, muscled hind legs, and ears longer than they were wide, was frozen mid-stride as though bounding up her forearm.

Her other tattoo, a skull flanked by an hourglass and a wilting flower in a vase, was on the inside of her other forearm. Beneath that sat her newest illustration she had inked last week. Words in small, italic script: *Don't fear what you can't see.* Ironic, given that all her fears now were not hidden. She saw them clearly every day.

The tattoo artist finished, then bound her arm in plastic wrap after wiping away the last of the blood.

The blood reminded her of that night, two months ago, high on the plateau at the top of the waterfall. For two weeks after, the police and the FBI had questioned her. She couldn't tell them much about those last fateful moments before she had passed out. The snake venom, like hot molten lead coursing through her veins, had made her delirious, dragging her into a semiconscious half world, filled with ghostly apparitions and fragmented voices. What she could remember, though, was the sensation of falling, then someone grabbing her arm and pulling her back. After that, she woke up in hospital where she spent several days recovering.

The authorities concluded that Dolores Gruber had stumbled and fallen to her own accidental death. With that part of the case closed, Emma Block was free to go.

The media soon labeled her, "The Girl That Got Away," while all she wanted was to be forgotten, to vanish into the background. Yesterday's news, not tomorrow's media obsession. So, she altered her appearance. Changed her name, too, and refused police protection. To herself, though, she would always be known as Emma.

She had briefly met an ex-FBI agent, Carolyn, who had visited her in the hospital that one time. Apparently, it was Carolyn who was instrumental in finding her and saving her. But the memories were still vague for Emma.

The nightmares, however, were clear and growing more frequent. Each night, Emma would wake to see him standing there in her bedroom, behind the thick curtain that was drawn across the window. His heavy work boots scuffed and scarred, the leather skin of one toe slit open like a scalpel wound, where part of the steel cap showing beneath would peek out from underneath. The folds of the curtain would billow ever so slightly, in and out, in time, with the labored sounds of his rasping breath. He said nothing, just stood there behind the curtain, waiting.

Emma had made amends with her mom. She also visited her father finally, who cried when he first saw her. That memory wasn't one to be locked away. Then she moved out of her home, and as far away as possible from the town of Camilla.

Outside the tattoo parlor, it was a beautiful, cloudless day, and the sun was shining brightly. Passing a store window, Emma caught sight of herself. She paused before turning her head left, then right, admiring the new person she saw.

Her once-blonde hair was now dyed raven black, cut into a modernistic chin-length blunt bob with bangs. Boyish, perhaps, but she liked it. It was a look that she hadn't seen in a fashion magazine or on a television shampoo commercial. It was a style, and a look that just came to her.

Emma continued walking.

In this town, her new home, no one knew, the girl that got away.

She did question if she really did "get away" from anything. For Emma, her memories were not memories at all. They were as real as the life she was now living every second of every day. It never went away. The father and daughter. The ranger. Dolores Gruber. And... him. Always him, behind her bedroom curtain. He was the only constant in her life. In every room she walked into. Every café she had coffee in. In every store she would browse in. At the parks she would visit and sit on a bench and just think and be alone. Emma would always catch a glimpse of him. Him across the street. Him riding past in the black pickup truck.

He was not an apparition, a figment of her imagination. He existed. With every breath she took, and every blink she made, he was watching her.

She hadn't wet her bed since she was a toddler. Now, washing the sheets had become her morning ritual. She slept with a gun. Ate with a gun. Went nowhere without being armed. And because she was only eighteen, Emma had to get a special permit. And like her change of name, the authorities granted it quickly, knowing the history of, the girl that got away.

52

RECOLLECTIONS

The days are getting longer, and hotter too. Summer is nearly here and spring almost gone.

The sand feels warm under my feet as I walk along the water's edge, the sky above me a brilliant hazy blue, the sun a blinding orb, the promise of scorching days and balmy nights ahead.

Over the last two months, I have thought about Emma a lot, wondering how she is, both physically and mentally. Her body will heal, but her mind may not.

Scratching my head, my hand comes away with a few more strands of hair. They ripple like fine ribbons in the morning breeze, curling around my fingertips as I regard them. I finally let them go, and they vanish into the shimmering haze, part of me, fading from view, disappearing piece by piece.

Beatriz hasn't discovered anything more about the two missing classmates of Emma's. It's an anomaly that I can't shake. There's something there, in the background of that young woman, slightly out of frame that I can't quite bring into focus.

We all have dark sides, I guess.

Beatriz is preoccupied with another case but is still searching for Pritchard when she can. The trail has gone beyond cold, though.

There's been no sign of him, and no other women have been abducted and killed that can be attributed to his MO. Or if there has, the FBI aren't releasing the information to the public. Maybe Wood and Miller figured out we accessed their computer files. Beatriz did mention the other day about a new firewall the FBI has installed, an extra layer of protection that she'll try to crack again. She's been hired to track down another killer, and it's taking up a lot of her time. Apparently, a multiple murderer, a woman called Victoria Christie has escaped from New York City, killed two prison guards and is on the run.

There's been no word from the authorities in Georgia, to see if they're going to lay charges against me for obstruction. Lucky me.

Things are on pause with me at the moment while I take care of myself.

As expected, the FBI has taken all credit for finding Emma. I don't care. Life goes on—or not.

When I visited her that one time in the hospital, I gave Emma my personal cell phone number. Told her not to tell anyone, and if she wanted to give me a call anytime, that she could, just to talk. That's the hardest part in a situation like that, finding someone you can talk to. I don't mean a shrink or friend or family member. They wouldn't understand. They have not experienced what I have. You need that bond, that shared suffering where you can look each other in the eye and just know.

But I have not heard from her. Aaron Wood and Dan Miller have ghosted me too.

The ocean is flat, glittering like an expanse of crushed glass. In the distance a container ship inches along the watery flatness.

I haven't been down into my basement office at all since I've been back. I can still see the wall of faces, though. It's hard not to. Pritchard is now the most wanted person in the entire country, and there's a nationwide manhunt for him.

Every day I've been walking along the beach, alone with my

thoughts, reliving those moments where I tried to kill him, smash his brains out with a rock. It was the right choice, even if it meant letting him escape. I saved Emma. And yet over the past weeks, doubt has crept into my mind. How many more women will he go on and kill? At that moment, on that ledge, I didn't think about it. All I thought about was saving the life that I could.

Reaching a small rock pool, I sit down and dip my toes into the clear water and tilt my face skyward, basking in the warmth of the sun on my pale skin. Before I was spending too many hours in my basement office, staring at the dead.

Closing my eyes, I think back to Emma, knowing that I'll never see her again. Who can blame her? I became a recluse. I imagine she's gone into hiding, changed her name, even her look.

I did read some of the newspapers where they labeled her as, "The Girl That Got Away." Nightmares, however, always manage to find you. And Sam Pritchard always leaves his indelible stain, like pure acid on your skin, on those who go on living in his murderous wake. Family, loved ones, friends, any person the deceased had touched when they were alive.

Emma is a clever girl.

I knew Pritchard had a gun. Standing that close to him, without him hearing my approach, I could just see it sticking out from the back of his waistband. Even with the gun, I was willing to take the chance, and attack him. Then I heard Emma bargaining with him, convincing him to toss the gun away. Standing there in the shadows, listening to their exchange, listening to her trying to negotiate her way out of what seemed like a hopeless situation gave me a newfound respect for her. She has courage, is a real fighter, willing to do whatever it takes. In a sense, she reminds me of how I was at her age. I bet she's a little hotheaded too.

When he tossed the gun, I pounced. I have her to thank for tilting the odds in my favor. Of course, my memory was a little patchy when I was interviewed by Wood and Miller.

It's a pity I didn't have the strength in those final moments to finish him off sooner. I was weakened, nauseous, my body just couldn't finish him even though my mind wanted so desperately to kill him. Killing the devil wasn't going to be easy. He is as resilient as he is cunning. He simply didn't crawl away and die in the wilderness from his injuries. He is very much alive. Even though I can't see him, he is always there, stalking me in my dreams and during my waking hours.

My third round of radiation therapy will be in a few weeks. The doctor says the initial signs are promising, though I need it to run its full course for the next few months. Can I commit to that knowing that he is still out there? He'll surface eventually. I know it. And when he does, I doubt if he would have mellowed by my actions. There have been times when I have thought about that, how the monster will be when he emerges from his cave. Inadvertently, by my actions in not killing him when I had the chance, I may have made him worse. He'll be seeking revenge, filthy with hatred, deranged with contempt. And when he can't take that out on me, I fear he'll take it out on other women, and he will probably escalate.

The breeze picks up, and another loose strand of hair gets taken by it, curling and spinning away.

Can I finish what I started? I thought I could. I'm not so sure now if I can do this on my own, if I can find and finish him off before the thing inside my head finishes me off.

I'll try. That's all I can really do.

And the police won't find him no matter how many resources they throw at it.

You send a loner to kill a loner.

It's not a case, either, of the police getting lucky, Pritchard being pulled over for a traffic stop, or someone recognizing him and making a citizen's arrest.

My days are now spent walking on the beach and reading in the afternoon with a glass of red wine on the back porch as the sun sets.

And in my periphery, a rancid evil blemish lurks. A dark sentinel is watching over me and waiting.

Standing, I walk back along the sand toward the wooden stairs at the base of the cliffs, gulls wheeling high above me.

My cell phone chimes. I glance at the screen while my hand instinctively goes straight to my gun in a holster concealed under my loose shirt.

The motion sensor camera set up on my front porch has been just triggered. Shading my eyes, I glance up at the cliff top. Someone is there, right now, outside my front door.

Activating the live stream from the camera, I watch. Someone is standing on my porch, but their head is tilted down. Suddenly they look up and stare straight at the camera in the corner of the ceiling.

My heart heaves in my chest, and confusion hits me as I stare at the stranger at my door.

53

NORTH STAR

The drive didn't take long. Three hours at the most.

Emma parked the car she had bought secondhand, her father having given her some of the money toward it. She then followed the path as it meandered through the sand dunes. After a five-minute walk, the beach house came into view, high on the bluff overlooking a small beach.

The Township of Erin's Bay lay two miles farther north, nestled on a crescent-shaped stretch of sandy coastline.

Cautiously, Emma climbed the porch stairs and noticed a small fish-eye security camera peering down at her from one corner. Undeterred, she knocked on the door, then stepped back and waited.

Behind the door came the sound of rattling chains and the turning of locks, almost as many locks as Emma had on her front door, she thought.

The door opened a few inches, and cold, flinty eyes peered out.

Looking at the face, Emma saw her own face staring back at her. *She's having the same nightmares as I am.*

The door opened wider to reveal a woman. Her posture was rigid, her shoulders tense, her face hard and gaunt. A gun held in one hand hung loosely by her side. The woman's cold gaze narrowed as she looked at Emma. After what seemed like an eternity, the woman's expression thawed slightly, but her face still kept its underlying hardness. "I can't say I like the new look," she said, appraising Emma's hair. Lifting her shirt, she slid the gun into a small holster on her belt, then covered it again with the shirt.

"Caroly—"

"No," the woman cut Emma off, holding up her hand.

"Please, just hear me out."

The woman shook her head vehemently. "I know what you're going to say."

"I can help you." Expecting initial resistance, Emma had rehearsed for this exact moment a thousand times on the drive up. What she would say, and how she would say it. She knew that she didn't want to kick off the conversation by asking for help, even though it was *she* who desperately needed it. The opposite approach would be better. By offering to help the woman, the woman would indirectly help Emma slay her own demon. The demon that they both now shared.

"No, you can't help," the woman said. Then the tension in her shoulders faded, and the door opened a little wider. Not enough, though, for the woman to step out, or for Emma to step through. "Look, Emma. You survived. No one else has. Don't ruin it. It is a gift from God, your life. Do not waste it on this." Her eyes shifted to the plastic wrap on Emma's forearm. Then a faint smile appeared among the hard edges of her cheekbones and jaw. "What did you get?"

Emma tilted her arm and peeled away enough of the plastic wrap for the woman to see.

"Nice." She looked up at Emma. More of the hard edges had melted away. "I always thought that's what you looked like when I first saw you bounding away from the entrance of that fallout shelter." The woman scratched her brow, like she was thinking, undecided, her posture less combative.

There was a faint crack there, in the woman's armor plating, and Emma decided to drive a wedge into it, and tell her everything. But instead of a calm, composed voice, as she had also practiced on the drive up, it came out in a spume of frustration, pent-up anger, and choked-back sobs. "I can't sleep. I wet my bed nearly every night. I'm having nightmares, and he is always there, in them. Every waking hour. Everywhere I go, I see him. I can't go on living like this," Emma pleaded, feeling tears, hot and sticky, running down her cheeks. "It's not how I want the rest of my life to be. We're all dying. It just seems like I'm dying faster than I'm supposed to be." She took a step closer. "He didn't kill me, but it's like he is slowly killing me now."

The woman wavered. Her seemingly hard exterior cracking some more. "How did you find me?" she asked.

"I asked around at the hospital after you left, and also one of the agents."

"But no one knows where I live."

"I'm good at finding people." Emma took another step forward. "And like I said, I can help. You may know more about him than me, but I've spent more time with him than you ever have." Emma waited, hoping the woman would understand. She had told no one what she was about to say next. "And..."

The woman looked at her, waiting for her to continue.

Emma's voice caught in her throat. "A...and...I've been having thoughts lately."

The woman jolted, like she had just received an electric shock. She tilted her head at Emma. "What kind of thoughts?"

Emma capitulated, unsure if she should tell her about this. She looked away, too ashamed to face the woman's questioning gaze. "Suicidal thoughts."

Emma turned back. Through her own tears, she saw the woman's tears—and more. Something solid and raw now shone behind the glassiness. *You know, don't you? You know what it is like.*

Maybe she had been there, too, as Emma had been. When all her options blinked out one by one, when she just wanted to escape the bottomless well of darkness that her life had become. At first, the cost, the exchange needed to climb out, was a currency too unimaginable for Emma to even contemplate. Then, as the well got deeper, and the despair began drowning her, and the circle of light above her shrank to a pinprick, the cost, the price, suddenly became more palatable. Her life.

Wiping away the tears with the back of her hand, Carolyn Ryder stepped aside and opened the door fully. She gestured. "Come inside, Emma."

Emma took a deep, welcoming breath. There was no turning back now.

And as she stepped across the threshold, the pinprick of light above her head seemed to shine slightly brighter.

Her means of escape had just become her North Star.

Turn the page for a FREE eBook

and

A SUMMER'S KILL,

Book #3 in The Killing Seasons

and

MURDER SCHOOL where you will learn more about Beatriz Vega, Carolyn's cyber-genius friend who has her hands full trying to hunt down a group of college students terrorizing New York City in a deadly game.

It's summer, and a cunning, demented killer is rising.

Carolyn Ryder made a choice that she may come to regret. It's been three months now since her near-death encounter with the country's most wanted Sam Pritchard, and still no sign of him. Returning to the coastal haven of Erin's Bay, she soon catches the unwanted attention of the new Deputy Chief of Police, Clayton Morelli. He's more than a little curious about the woman who lives in the beach house high on the clifftops.

Then there is the town's newest resident, Ellie Sutton. A mysterious young woman with an uncertain past who lives down by the boat harbor. Ellie avoids attention at every turn — that is until she puts a burly trawlerman into the local hospital with a broken arm.

Despite Pritchard's vanishing act, Carolyn knows he's not finished with her. Like a slow, creeping death, he's out there, somewhere, watching and waiting to enact his revenge.

It's summer, but something cold and murderous is lurking in the shadows of the township.

The worst thing you can do is try to kill a serial killer... and fail.

A Summer's Kill is available through Amazon in paperback, kindle and kindle unlimited

Present-day Hunger Games meets The Talented 'Miss' Ripley, with a dose of Law & Order

A convicted ex-cop who has lost everything. A rogue female detective desperate to save her city. An agoraphobic computer genius who hunts monsters for a living. And a brilliant forensic pathologist who is deadly with a scalpel. Four unlikely heroes are thrown together to hunt down and save New York from a group of murderous super-villains' intent on killing as many people as possible.

Catching killers is nothing new for Homicide Detective, Eve Sommers —until she begins to see a disturbing pattern emerge in a series of seemingly random murders at famous New York City landmarks.

Teaming up with her friend, Dr. Maya Zin, a brilliant forensic pathologist, Eve soon discovers that a group of Ivy League college students are playing a deadly game to commit the most audacious, most public murders they can. Eve will stop at nothing to protect her city and catch the killers, even if it means ending up on their 'Murder Bucket List'.

Two years ago, NYPD cop Thomas Birch was sent to prison by his own colleagues for a crime he didn't commit. Now out, Birch struggles to find any meaning in his life—that is until Francis Latimer, a reclusive billionaire offers him one last chance at redemption. In exchange for irrefutable evidence of his innocence, Birch must first find Latimer's missing daughter, Lindsay. But tracking down Lindsay Latimer will be no easy task, when he discovers she is running with the same killers the police are now hunting.

Pitted against each other, corrupt forces within their own police department, and a group of murderous super-villains terrorizing the city, Eve and Birch race to find Lindsay Latimer, and uncover the truth. Is she really the perfect daughter everyone thinks? Or is she something truly evil?

Murder School is available through Amazon in paperback, kindle and kindle unlimited

Young man helps desperate woman from being bullied off her ranch by a ruthless small-town family.

In the small town of Martha's End, Kansas, trouble is brewing. Two feuding families, the McAlister's and the Morgan's have been in conflict for generations, and Ben Shaw, a young and good looking man, soon finds himself caught in the middle.

With the Morgan family patriarch, Jim Morgan, ruling the town with his three sons, and dark and sinister things happening on the Morgan ranch, Daisy McAlister, the last of the McAlister family bloodline, is in need of help. But with his unique skillset and mysterious past, Ben Shaw may be the one to tip the balance in her favor.

Will justice be served in this town or will it take a higher power? Find out in this suspenseful thriller novel.

ALSO AVAILABLE BY JK ELLEM

Audrey Kills Again!

Taxi Man

Murder School

Deadly Touch Series

Fast Read - Deadly Touch

Octagon Trilogy (Dystopian Thriller Series)

Prequel - Soldiers Field

Book 1 - Octagon

Book 2 - Infernum

Book 3 - Sky of Thorns

Boxsets

No Justice Box Set 1

Deadly Touch, No Justice, Cold Justice

No Justice Box Set 2

American Justice, Hidden Justice, Raw Justice

Ben Shaw Road Trip Thriller Box Set 1

Fast Justice, Sinful Justice, Dark Justice

Octagon Box Set

Soldiers Field, Octagon, Infernum

JK Ellem was born in London and spent his formative years preferring to read books and comics rather than doing his homework.

He is the innovative author of short chapter, Hitchcock-style adult thrillers in the genres of crime, mystery, and psychological thrillers which have multiple plot lines that culminate in explosive, unpredictable endings that will leave you shocked.

In 2022 he was accepted into the Curtis Brown Creative, Writing Your Novel in Six Months course which he undertook in London while working on his manuscript for future submission.

He splits his time between the US, the UK and Australia.

Printed in Great Britain
by Amazon

32826191R00142